WINDJAMMER WORLD

A DOWN EAST GALLEY-EYE VIEW

SKETCHES AND TEXT

BY

DEE CARSTARPHEN

ISBN 0-89272-066-2
9 8 7 6 5 4 3

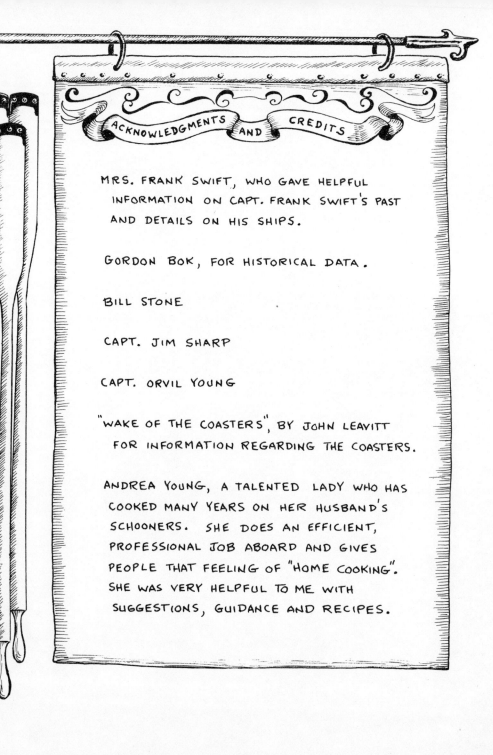

ACKNOWLEDGMENTS AND CREDITS

MRS. FRANK SWIFT, WHO GAVE HELPFUL
INFORMATION ON CAPT. FRANK SWIFT'S PAST
AND DETAILS ON HIS SHIPS.

GORDON BOK, FOR HISTORICAL DATA.

BILL STONE

CAPT. JIM SHARP

CAPT. ORVIL YOUNG

"WAKE OF THE COASTERS", BY JOHN LEAVITT
FOR INFORMATION REGARDING THE COASTERS.

ANDREA YOUNG, A TALENTED LADY WHO HAS
COOKED MANY YEARS ON HER HUSBAND'S
SCHOONERS. SHE DOES AN EFFICIENT,
PROFESSIONAL JOB ABOARD AND GIVES
PEOPLE THAT FEELING OF "HOME COOKING".
SHE WAS VERY HELPFUL TO ME WITH
SUGGESTIONS, GUIDANCE AND RECIPES.

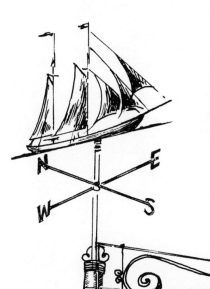

DEDICATED
TO ALL THOSE
GALLEY SLAVES WHO, THROUGH
THE LONG SUMMERS, HAVE
GIVEN THEIR ALL TO BE
PART OF THE
SAILING SHIP
AND HER
MYSTIQUE.

TO:

KATHY

BETH

BRIDGET

PEANUT

AND PAT

INDEX

CAKES

ALMOND CAKE	88
APPLECAKE	89
APPLESAUCE SPICE	89
BLUEBERRY PUDDING CAKE	89
CARROT NUT CAKE	90
CHEESECAKE	104
CHEESECAKE, PUMPKIN	104
CHOCOLATE CAKE	91
FRUIT COCKTAIL CAKE	90
GINGERBREAD	90
HUNDRED DOLLAR CAKE	86
MARLIN SPIKE CAKE	86
PINEAPPLE UPSIDE DOWN CAKE	88
POUND CAKE	81
SHORTCAKE	69
SPONGE CAKE, HOT MILK	87

FROSTINGS

BOILED WHITE	87
CHOCOLATE	91

DESSERT SAUCES

BUTTERSCOTCH	102
CHOCOLATE # 1	102
CHOCOLATE # 2	102
LEMON, QUICK	91
PUDDING OR CAKE SAUCE	91

COOKIES

BROWNIES	95
BUTTERSCOTCH FRUIT BARS	95

EGG DISHES

SALADS

SALAD DRESSINGS

SANDWICHES

STUFFINGS

SOUPS AND CHOWDERS

PUMPKIN SOUP 125
TOMATO BISQUE 124

LUNCHEON HOT POTS

CHICKEN OR TURKEY LOAF 129
CHILE 126
HAM LOAF 129
LASAGNA 127
MEAT LOAF 129
MEXICALI BAKE 126
PIZZA 128
RED FLANNEL HASH 128
SPAGHETTI SAUCE 127
STIR FRIED RICE 127

MEAT, FOWL AND FISH

BEEF 130
CHICKEN, COUNTRY 132
CHICKEN, OVEN FRIED 132
CHICKEN, MANDARIN 132
CHICKEN, SHERRIED 132
CORNED BEEF 134
FISH, "AH SO" 131
FISH, BAKED HADDOCK 132
FISH, FLORENTINE 130
FISH, MACADAMIA 131
FISH, OVEN FRIED 131
HAM 131
LAMB 130
NEW ENGLAND BOILED DINNER 134
PORK . . . . , . . 130
TURKEY 130

MEAT SAUCES

VEGETABLES

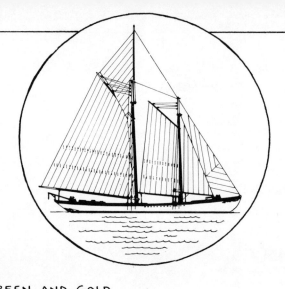

VEGETABLE SAUCES

THE LAST OF SIXTEEN THOUSAND SHIPS*
   NOW SAIL UPON THE BAY,
AND CARRY SUMMER VISITORS
   ONE HALF A WORLD AWAY.

THE REMNANTS OF A SCHOONER FLEET,
   THE SKIN BOATS ARE THE LAST
TO SAIL FROM HAPPY SUMMER PORTS
   INTO A GOLDEN PAST.

THE CARGO IN EACH AMPLE HOLD
   IS DREAMS INSTEAD OF LIME,
OR PULP, OR SHAKES, OR MERCHANDISE
   FROM SOME FAR DISTANT TIME.

SO RAISE THE TOPS'L TO THE BREEZE,
   OR SUMMON UP A GALE,
AND SAIL AWAY TO YESTERDAY
   AND THE GOLDEN DAYS OF SAIL.

                    JAMES RUSSELL WIGGINS

*16,000 schooners were
sighted off Owls Head in 1876.

WINDJAMMER WORLD

By Dee Carstarphen

ALL UP AND DOWN THE EASTERN COAST, FROM NANTUCKET TO PENOBSCOT BAY, A DOZEN OR MORE WINDJAMMERS PLY THEIR TRADE DURING THE SUMMER MONTHS. A WINDJAMMER IS A VESSEL THAT WORKS UNDER SAIL, AND SINCE THE 1930's, THE TERM HAS APPLIED TO LARGE SAILING SHIPS THAT TAKE PASSENGERS FOR HIRE ON A "HEAD" BASIS. THESE VESSELS THAT WORK THE BAYS AND SOUNDS OF THE UNITED STATES ARE COAST GUARD INSPECTED EVERY SPRING, THEIR CAPTAINS ARE LICENSED, AND THEY MAKE CRUISES OF A WEEK'S DURATION. MOST OF THESE SHIPS ARE PURE SAILING VESSELS WITH NO INBOARD ENGINES AND MUST DEPEND UPON WIND AND TIDE

WHEN UNDER WAY. CONSEQUENTLY, CRUISES HAVE NO REGULAR ROUTE. AND A SHIP MAY SAIL THE COASTLINE EITHER TOWARDS MT. DESERT ISLE OR BOOTHBAY.

1

THE MAJORITY OF THESE WINDJAMMERS HAIL FROM
MAINE. ROCKPORT AND ROCKLAND ARE HOME PORTS
FOR A FEW SHIPS, BUT CAMDEN IS THE BUSIEST WIND-
JAMMER CENTER, THE PICTURESQUE LITTLE HARBOR SPROUTING
MASTS FROM NO LESS THAN SEVEN VESSELS --- A GRAND
AND GLORIOUS SIGHT ON A SUMMER WEEKEND TO DROP
DOWN OVER THE HILL AND SEE A HOST OF SPARS AND
RIGGING RISING OVER THE ROOFTOPS, FLAGS
FLYING IN THE BREEZE.

HOW DID IT ALL START?

IN THE EARLY 1930'S A MAN NAMED
FRANK SWIFT WAS

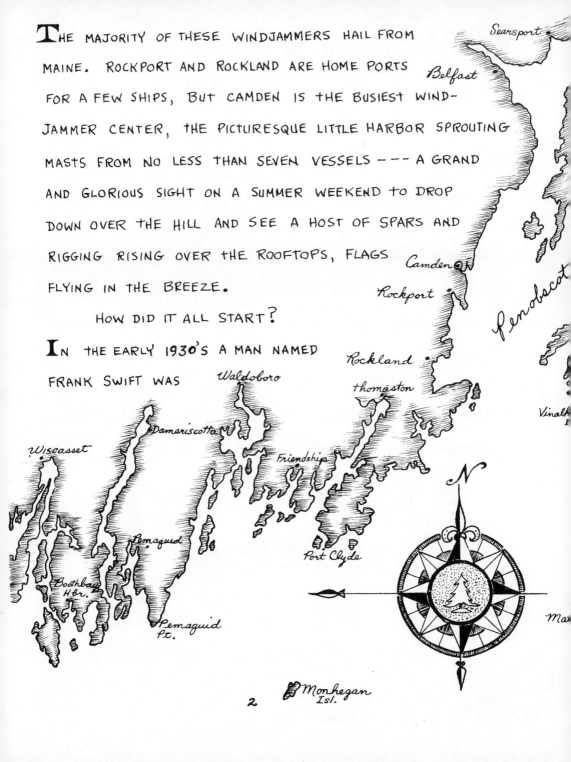

Searsport

Belfast

Camden

Rockport

Penobscot

Rockland

Waldoboro

Thomaston

Vinal

Damariscotta

Wiscasset

Friendship

Pemaquid

Port Clyde

Boothbay Hbr.

Pemaquid Pt.

N

Ma

Monhegan Isl.

ASSOCIATED WITH A BOYS' SUMMER CAMP IN

MAINE AND BECAME ACQUAINTED WITH CAPT.

PARKER HALL OF SANDY POINT.   CAPT. HALL

WAS ONE OF THE LEGENDARY CAPTAINS ACTIVE IN THE NEW ENGLAND

COASTING TRADE.*   SWIFT SAILED WITH CAPT. HALL AND ARRANGED

---

* Coasters were sailing craft carrying cargoes from one coastal port to another — not considered deep-water vessels, their hey-day was the mid 1800's until World War I, before good roads were built and weather conditions made coastal towns inaccessible a large part of the year.

3

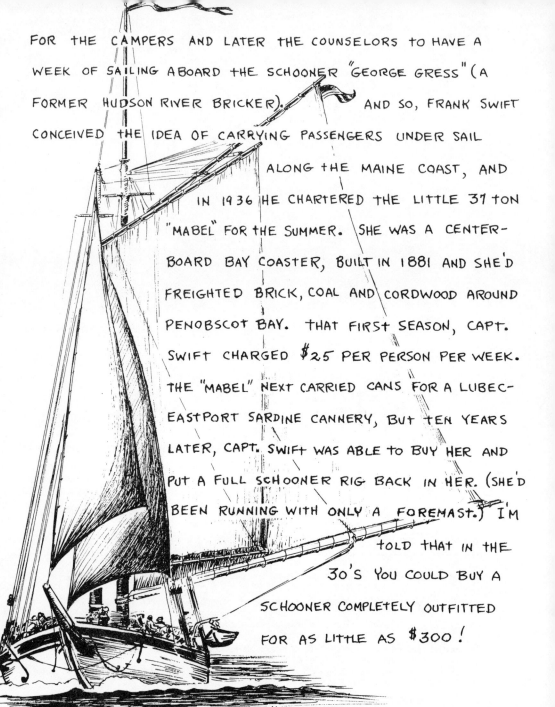

FOR THE CAMPERS AND LATER THE COUNSELORS TO HAVE A WEEK OF SAILING ABOARD THE SCHOONER "GEORGE GRESS" (A FORMER HUDSON RIVER BRICKER). AND SO, FRANK SWIFT CONCEIVED THE IDEA OF CARRYING PASSENGERS UNDER SAIL ALONG THE MAINE COAST, AND IN 1936 HE CHARTERED THE LITTLE 37 TON "MABEL" FOR THE SUMMER. SHE WAS A CENTER-BOARD BAY COASTER, BUILT IN 1881 AND SHE'D FREIGHTED BRICK, COAL AND CORDWOOD AROUND PENOBSCOT BAY. THAT FIRST SEASON, CAPT. SWIFT CHARGED $25 PER PERSON PER WEEK. THE "MABEL" NEXT CARRIED CANS FOR A LUBEC-EASTPORT SARDINE CANNERY, BUT TEN YEARS LATER, CAPT. SWIFT WAS ABLE TO BUY HER AND PUT A FULL SCHOONER RIG BACK IN HER. (SHE'D BEEN RUNNING WITH ONLY A FOREMAST.) I'M TOLD THAT IN THE 30'S YOU COULD BUY A SCHOONER COMPLETELY OUTFITTED FOR AS LITTLE AS $300!

IN 1937 AND 1938, CAPT. SWIFT CHARTERED THE SCHOONER "LYDIA M. WEBSTER", WHICH HE LATER OWNED. THE FIRST VESSEL HE BOUGHT (1938) WAS THE "ANNIE F. KIMBALL" (A WELL-KNOWN PACKET AND BAY COASTER). IMAGINE THE PERSEVERANCE, ENDEAVOR AND IMAGINATION IT MUST HAVE TAKEN FOR THIS MAN TO BUILD A FLEET TO AS MANY AS TWELVE SHIPS—MOST OF THEM OLD MAINE WORKING SCHOONERS. HE CONVERTED THEM FROM CARGO OR FISHING VESSELS INTO WHAT THE OLD-TIMERS CALL "DUDE CRUISERS". IN THE PROCESS, IT WAS NECESSARY TO SOMETIMES MAKE MAJOR REPAIRS, AND LARGE SUMS WERE SPENT TO MAINTAIN THEM OVER THE 25 YEARS HE WAS IN THE BUSINESS.

A REMARKABLE MAN, CAPT. SWIFT GREW UP IN DUTCHESS COUNTY, NEW YORK AND LEARNED HIS SEAMANSHIP AND SAILING AS A CADET ON THE NEW YORK STATE MERCHANT MARINE SCHOOL SHIP, THE BARKENTINE "NEWPORT". AT ONE TIME HE MADE A VOYAGE TO THE ORIENT AS CREW ON A BARBER LINE FREIGHTER. HE WAS AN ACCOMPLISHED ARTIST, WITH A FORMAL EDUCATION IN PAINTING AND SILVERSMITHING. HE WAS A PROFESSIONAL SCENIC DESIGNER AND PAINTER FOR SEVEN YEARS AND ALSO CREATED SILVER AND PEWTER HOLLOW AND

"Oh, Camden is a fine town, with ships about the bay —"

FLATWEAR AND GOLD AND SILVER JEWELRY. HE WAS ESPECIALLY ENAMORED OF THE MAINE COASTAL WATERS AND THE COASTING SCHOONERS. EACH SUMMER HE WENT AS MASTER ON ONE OF HIS VESSELS.

HIS SHIPS WERE : 1. "MABEL"   2. "LYDIA M. WEBSTER"

3. "ANNIE F. KIMBALL"   4. "ENTERPRISE"   5. "EVA S. CULLISON"

6. "CLINTON"   7. "LOIS M. CANDAGE"   8. "LILLIAN"

9. "MATTIE" (ORIGINALLY NAMED "GRACE BAILEY") WAS BUILT IN 1882 AT PATCHOGUE, LONG ISLAND. A WIDE, SHOAL CENTERBOARDER, SHE SAILED AT FIRST WITH THE BOXBOARD FLEET. ✻   SHE ALSO SAILED THE WEST INDIES FRUIT TRADE. SHE'S STILL OPERATING OUT OF CAMDEN UNDER CAPT. LES BEX.   10. "MERCANTILE" IS 78 FT. AND WAS BUILT AT DEER ISLE IN 1916. SHE WAS OPERATED AS A

✻ *Boxboards were rough planks. The bark was still on the boards and they had to be handled one at a time. It was hard on the hands and the uneven edges didn't stow as closely as finished lumber.*

6

PACKET AND IS ALSO SAILING TODAY UNDER CAPT. BEX. 11. "INDRA" WAS A YACHT PUT INTO SERVICE. 12. "YANKEE", IRVING JOHNSON'S DUTCH PILOT BOAT IN WHICH HE TOOK STUDENT GROUPS AROUND THE WORLD. SHE WAS LESS SUITED TO COASTWISE SAILING THAN TO DEEP WATER VOYAGES, WHICH LED TO CAPT. SWIFT'S SELLING HIS INTEREST IN HER. SHE SAILED NOVA SCOTIA WATERS FOR A FEW YEARS AND FINALLY SANK OFF CAPE BRETON.

SOME OF THE CAPTAINS NOW SUCCESSFUL IN THE HEAD BOAT BUSINESS HAVE GROWN UP WITH IT. THEY ARE USUALLY AS INTER-ESTING AS THEIR VESSELS. CAPT. BOYD GUILD BROUGHT THE "STEPHEN TABER" INTO THE TRADE. THE "TABER" WAS BUILT IN 1871 IN LONG ISLAND SOUND. SHE CARRIED BRICKS AND CEMENT ON THE HUDSON RIVER. SHE WAS COMPLETELY REBUILT IN THE 30'S AND USED IN THE PULPWOOD BUSINESS UNTIL CAPT. GUILD CHANGED HER LIFE. HE, IN TURN, SOLD HER TO CAPT. HAVILAH HAWKINS, WHO RAN HER SUC-CESSFULLY FOR MANY A YEAR. CAPT. JIM SHARP OPERATED THE "TABER" FOR A SEASON AND CAPT. ORVIL YOUNG HAD HER TEN YEARS BEFORE SELLING HER. SHE IS STILL OWNER-OPERATED. SHE'S STARTED A LOT OF SKIPPERS IN THE BUSINESS AND IS KNOWN AS A GOOD LUCK SHIP.

THEN THERE WAS THE "ALICE WENTWORTH"! MANY DOWN-EASTERN SAILORS HELD A SOFT SPOT FOR HER.

BUILT AT SOUTH NORWALK AS THE "LIZZIE A. TOLLES" IN 1863, SHE WAS A VERY PRETTY COASTER WITH A LOVELY DEEP SHEER. SHE WAS WELL-KNOWN FOR HER SAILING ABILITY.

CAPT. GUILD OWNED AND RAN HER AND SO DID CAPT. HAWKINS. SHE CAME UPON HARD TIMES AND ENDED HER DAYS AS A TOURIST AT-TRACTION ON THE BOSTON WATERFRONT, SINKING AND BEING RAISED A FEW TIMES BEFORE THEY LET HER BONES LIE.

THE "MARVEL" WAS A CENTERBOARD CHESAPEAKE BAY RAM. IN THE FALL OF 1955 SHE WAS CARRYING PASSENGERS ON A SAILING TRIP IN THE CHESAPEAKE AREA. SHE'D BEEN UP THE CHOPTANK AND THOUGH THEY'D HEARD A STORM WAS APPROACHING, THE WEATHER WAS BEAUTIFUL AND THEY'D BEEN LULLED INTO STAYING FOR A SWIM. TOO LATE! SHE RAN ACROSS THE BAY AND WAS CAUGHT BY A HURRICANE

8

IN AN EXPOSED AREA WITH SHOAL WATERS. SHE ANCHORED OFF HOLLAND Pt. AND THE WIND VEERED AROUND. THEY HAD NEITHER ENOUGH POWER NOR CREW AND THE GALE DROVE HER ONTO THE BAR. SHE WAS BEAM TO THE HURRICANE FORCE WIND, WHICH HEELED HER DOWN AND CRESTING SEAS POURED ABOARD. SOME SMALL BOATS WORKED OUT FROM SHORE TO SAVE LIVES. A FEW TRIED TO SWIM AND DROWNED. TWELVE OR FOURTEEN PEOPLE WERE LOST AND THIS DISASTER RESULTED IN THE COAST GUARD AMENDING SAFETY RULES AND REGULATIONS GOVERNING SAILING CRAFT CARRYING

PASSENGERS FOR HIRE — RULES STILL IN EFFECT TODAY. THEY'RE DIFFERENT FROM THE REGULATIONS PERTAINING TO MOTOR VESSELS.

SOME VESSELS NOW IN OPERATION:
THE "VICTORY CHIMES" WAS BUILT IN 1900 IN BETHEL, DELAWARE. A 132 FT. CENTERBOARD RAM, SHE CARRIED CARGOES THROUGH THE CHESAPEAKE AND DELAWARE CANAL. SHE WAS OPERATING IN THE CHESAPEAKE AREA THE SAME TIME AS THE "MARVEL". SHE RUNS OUT OF ROCKLAND UNDER CAPT. BOYD GUILD.

9

CAPT. HAVILAH (BUDS) HAWKINS HAD THE "MARY DAY" BUILT IN 1962. SHE'S AN 83 FT. CENTERBOARD SCHOONER, THE FIRST OF HER TYPE TO BE BUILT IN 30 YEARS AND SPECIFICALLY TO CARRY PASSENGERS UNDER SAIL.

SINCE THAT TIME, A FEW OTHER VESSELS HAVE BEEN SPECIALLY BUILT — THE "SHENANDOAH" (MARTHA'S VINEYARD), THE "BILL OF RIGHTS" (NEWPORT, R.I.) AND THE "HARVEY GAMAGE". THE "GAMAGE" RUNS OUT OF ROCKLAND IN THE SUMMER AND SAILS TO THE CARIBBEAN FOR THE WINTER SEASON. THESE SHIPS WERE ALL BUILT IN THE GAMAGE YARD IN SOUTH BRISTOL. NOW, WITH ESCALATING COSTS, **THE DAYS OF BUILDING WOODEN SCHOONERS FOR THE TRADE ARE NUMBERED.** THE CHANCE OF MAKING BACK THE COST OF A VESSEL IN HER LIFETIME IS RAPIDLY BECOMING AN IMPOSSIBILITY.

SOME OLD SHIPS HAVE BEEN FOUND AND BROUGHT BACK. IN ROCKLAND AT THE NORTH END SHIPYARD THERE HAVE BEEN SOME FINE RESTORATIONS.

THE "LEWIS R. FRENCH" WAS

10

BUILT IN CHRISTMAS COVE IN 1871 AND HAD BEEN RUN AS A
FISHING SCHOONER; SHE ALSO CARRIED FREIGHT ALONG THE
COAST. AN EXPLOSION IN THE EARLY TWENTIES HAD WRECKED
HER. SHE WAS LATER REBUILT AND USED AS A CANNERY
LIGHTER. NOW SHE'S COMPLETELY REDONE AGAIN —
HANDSOMELY, AND IS RUNNING OUT OF ROCKLAND
UNDER HER OWNER, CAPT. JOHN FOSS.

THE "ISAAC H. EVANS" IS ANOTHER OLD-TIMER.
SHE'S 64 FT. (AS IS THE "FRENCH"), WAS BUILT IN
1886 IN MAURICETOWN, NEW JERSEY, AND SPENT
HER LIFE FREIGHTING AND OYSTERING ON
DELAWARE BAY. SHE CAME TO MAINE IN THE
EARLY 70'S AND WAS REBUILT AT A YARD IN
BATH, MAINE BY CAPT. DOUGLAS LEE TO CARRY PASSENGERS.

THE "TIMBERWIND" IS 70 FT. SHE WAS
BUILT IN PORTLAND, MAINE IN 1931. ORIGINALLY
NAMED "PORTLAND PILOT", SHE CARRIED
PILOTS OUT OF PORTLAND UNTIL 1969
WHEN SHE WAS REBUILT FOR WINDJAM-
MING. HER OWNER-CAPT. IS BILL
ALEXANDER. SHE'S FROM ROCKPORT.

11

The "J. & E. RIGGIN" IS A MORE RECENT ADDITION TO THE FLEET. AN 89 FT. CENTER-BOARDER, SHE WAS AN OYSTER SCHOONER ON DELAWARE BAY AND BUILT IN DORCHESTER, NEW JERSEY IN 1927.

CAPT. DAVE ALLEN HAS SPENT TWO YEARS RESTORING HER.

CAPT. JIM SHARP OWNS AND OPERATES THE 121 FT. GLOUCESTER SCHOONER "ADVENTURE". CAPT. SHARP HAD CUT HIS TEETH IN THE CHARTER BUSINESS IN THE BAHAMAS SAILING HIS "MALABAR" SCHOONER. WHEN HE MOVED TO MAINE, HE BOUGHT "STEPHEN TABER" AND RAN HER FOR A YEAR. HE WENT INTO PARTNERSHIP WITH CAPT. ORVIL YOUNG, WHO RAN THE "TABER" WHEN CAPT. SHARP BOUGHT THE "ADVENTURE" IN 1965. THE "ADVENTURE HAD BEEN SHORT RIGGED AND CAPT. SHARP WAS ABLE TO RESTORE THE VESSEL TO HER FULL RIG. SHE'S A GRAND SAILING SHIP TODAY.

"ADVENTURE" WAS BUILT IN ESSEX IN 1926 — A GLOUCESTER DORY FISHING "KNOCKABOUT", *

*Knockabout — without a bowsprit.

12

SHE FISHED UNTIL 1954 SO SUCCESSFULLY SHE WAS AN ALL
TIME "HIGH LINER" AND IS THE ONLY FISHING SCHOONER LEFT
SAILING TODAY. HER SLEEK HULL WAS BUILT FOR SPEED TO BRING
THE HADDOCK (IN THE WINTER) AND HALIBUT (IN THE SUMMER) FROM
THE BANKS, AND SHE WAS PROBABLY THE GREATEST PRODUCER
AND MONEY-MAKER IN THE HISTORY OF THE NORTH ATLANTIC FISHERIES.

CAPT. SHARP AND CAPT. YOUNG HAVE RECENTLY ACQUIRED THE
SCHOONER "ROSEWAY". SHE IS A 112 FT. GLOUCESTER SCHOONER
BUILT IN ESSEX AT THE SAME YARD AS THE "ADVENTURE",
ONE YEAR EARLIER. SHE WAS USED AS A YACHT AND FISHED
TOO UNTIL 1941 WHEN THE BOSTON PILOTS BOUGHT HER.
SHE WAS A PILOT BOAT INTO THE '70'S.
SHE'S COAST GUARD APPROVED WITH
AN AUXILIARY ENGINE AND HAS WATER-
TIGHT BULKHEADS THROUGHOUT. SHE
BEGAN SAILING PASSENGERS IN 1975
UNDER THE ABLE HAND OF CAPT.
ORVIL YOUNG. HE HAS ADDED NEW
TOPMASTS AND SHE'S EASILY
RECOGNIZED ON THE BAY BY
HER RED "TANBARK" SAILS.

13

CAPT. JIM SHARP WAS INSTRUMENTAL IN BRINGING THE 85 FT.
SCHOONER "BOWDOIN" TO MAINE. SHE WAS BUILT IN 1921 AND WAS
ADMIRAL MACMILLAN'S ARCTIC RESEARCH VESSEL. HE MADE TWENTY-
SIX VOYAGES OF EXPLORATION AND DISCOVERY ABOVE THE ARCTIC
CIRCLE WITH HER BEFORE GIVING HER TO MYSTIC SEAPORT MUSEUM
IN 1960. TEN YEARS LATER CAPT. SHARP BROUGHT HER TO
CAMDEN FOR REBUILDING. SHE HAS BEEN OPERATING AS A
PASSENGER VESSEL SINCE THAT TIME.

THE "MATTIE" AND THE "MERCANTILE" HAVE ALREADY BEEN
MENTIONED. THEIR HOME PORT IS CAMDEN AND THEY ARE
OWNED BY CAPT. LES BEX. HE ALSO OWNS THE 40 FT.
SCHOONER "MISTRESS", BUILT ON THE SAME LINES AS THE OLD
COASTERS. SHE DOES HAVE AN ENGINE AND CARRIES SIX
PASSENGERS. CAPT. BEX HAS DONE A TREMENDOUS
AMOUNT OF RESTORATION ON HIS SHIPS.

AN IMPRESSIVE LIST!

These ships probably carry four thousand passengers each season and no one has been killed or badly injured and no schooner damaged in the Penobscot Bay area in forty years. Considering the age of some of the vessels, that's a mighty good record! Most of these ships are owner-operated and their reputations, lives, and business depend on good sense. The grand old ships survive today because of great care.

deadeyes and lanyards

Each summer increasing numbers of sail-minded people come, some neophytes and some sailors, with the need to return for a short while to the basics of life on a large sailing ship. Nowhere else in the world can one find this particular unique kind of trip. More people than ever before are involved in various aspects of boating.

15

AS COMPETITIVE COMPANIES BUILD MORE AND MORE STOCK
TYPE PLASTIC BOATS, THE TREND IS TOWARDS LUXURY...
"BUY ME (OR RENT ME)", THEY PLEAD, "AND I'LL GIVE
YOU EVERYTHING YOU HAVE AT HOME TO MAKE YOU COMFY-
HI-FI AND STEREO, LARGER TANKS FOR WATER AND
FUEL, HOT WATER SHOWERS, REFRIGERATION AND DEEP
FREEZERS".   ALL OF WHICH MAKES GENERATORS AND
BACK UP SYSTEMS NECESSARY, AND SNOWBALLS THE
WHOLE AFFAIR INTO A TENSE "KEEP IT ALL RUNNING"
KIND OF OPERATION THAT PEOPLE WHO TAKE TO BOATING
HOPE TO GET AWAY FROM IN THE FIRST PLACE.

— BACK TO BASICS!

WHAT A DELIGHT FOR THE AVERAGE GUY TO PAY A
NOMINAL PRICE TO GO OUT ON A GRAND OLD SHIP AND
SHUCK AWAY THE LAYERS OF COMPLICATIONS INVOLVED WITH
THE MODERN ELECTRONIC WONDERS. OLD TRADITIONALISTS
MAY SNEER AT WHAT THEY CALL THE
"DUDE CRUISERS" AND SAY
THEY HAVE NO

RESEMBLANCE to HOW "IT REALLY WAS". MAYBE NOT! BUT IT
RETAINS THE FLAVOR OF THAT VANISHED AND ALMOST FORGOTTEN
WAY OF LIFE. A RETURN TO THE ERA OF NOSTALGIA.

It's A VERITABLE TREAT FOR THE SENSES — FOG, PINE
ISLANDS DARK AGAINST THEIR GRANITE BASES,
THAT ROCKY, TREE-CLAD COAST, THE SEA
IN ALL IT'S MOODS, SAILS
AND RIGGING,
SPACIOUS DECKS
AND THE SOUNDS OF
A WOODEN SHIP
CREAKING, WHIFF OF
WOOD SMOKE AND
STOCKHOLM TAR FROM
OAKUM AND MARLIN,
SALT AIR AND
FIR TREES,
BREAD BAKING,
A CLOSENESS TO
NATURE AND SHIPMATES — SHARED WORK AND
PLAY. TASTE BUDS FULL — FANTASTIC FOOD... FOOD!

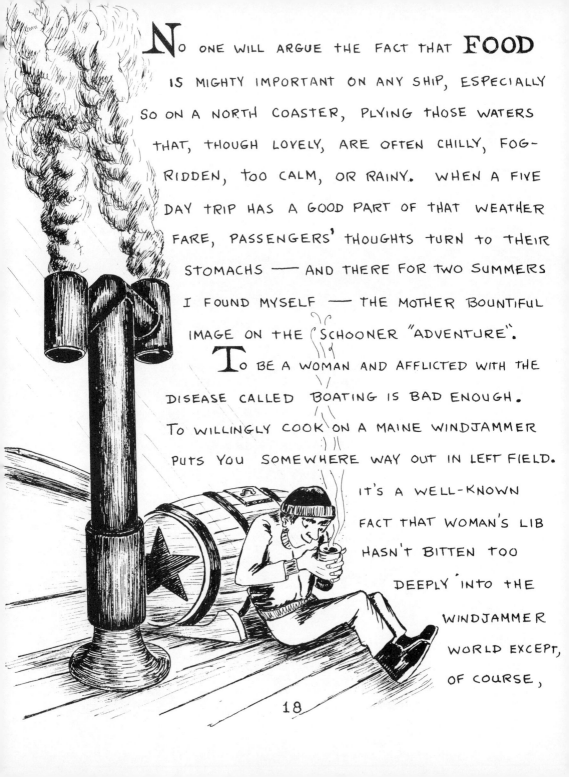

NO ONE WILL ARGUE THE FACT THAT **FOOD** IS MIGHTY IMPORTANT ON ANY SHIP, ESPECIALLY SO ON A NORTH COASTER, PLYING THOSE WATERS THAT, THOUGH LOVELY, ARE OFTEN CHILLY, FOG-RIDDEN, TOO CALM, OR RAINY. WHEN A FIVE DAY TRIP HAS A GOOD PART OF THAT WEATHER FARE, PASSENGERS' THOUGHTS TURN TO THEIR STOMACHS — AND THERE FOR TWO SUMMERS I FOUND MYSELF — THE MOTHER BOUNTIFUL IMAGE ON THE SCHOONER "ADVENTURE".

TO BE A WOMAN AND AFFLICTED WITH THE DISEASE CALLED BOATING IS BAD ENOUGH. TO WILLINGLY COOK ON A MAINE WINDJAMMER PUTS YOU SOMEWHERE WAY OUT IN LEFT FIELD.

IT'S A WELL-KNOWN FACT THAT WOMAN'S LIB HASN'T BITTEN TOO DEEPLY INTO THE WINDJAMMER WORLD EXCEPT, OF COURSE,

IN THAT TRADITIONAL LITTLE WOMAN'S ROLE OF COOK, DISH-
WASHER, POT-SCRUBBER, ETC.

Every SPRING THERE ARE A CERTAIN NUMBER OF
BRIGHT-EYED, EAGER FEMALES, WANTING TO EXPERIENCE
THE THRILL OF SAILING THROUGH THE BEAUTIFUL PINEY
ISLANDS OF PENOBSCOT BAY, AND HOPING TO BE PART OF
THE TRADITIONAL, ROMANTIC AND UNSPOILED FREE LIFE ON
THE LARGE VESSELS. WHEN YOU'RE HIRED ON, YOU <u>ARE</u>
PART OF IT, YOU BET! ...DOING YOUR THING DOWN IN
THE DARK GALLEY REGIONS — STOKING THE FIRE,
SWEATING PROFUSELY, TURNING OUT VAST QUANTITIES OF
"TYPICAL DOWNEAST" DELICACIES AND REFLECTING
ON WHICH DEMON OF THIS
PARTICULAR HELL HAS PRODDED
YOU INTO DOING THIS.

19

YOU SING AND LAUGH A LOT AND TRY TO PLAN THE MEALS
SO YOU CAN RUN TOPSIDE AND LOOK AROUND ONCE IN A WHILE.
THERE IS SOME TIME ON DECK AFTER LUNCH, BUT IT'S
QUESTIONABLE IF THAT COMPENSATES FOR RISING AT FIVE
A.M. AND FINALLY TAKING THE APRON OFF
AROUND EIGHT P.M. WHEN FOLKS MARVEL
AT WHAT YOU'RE DOING, YOU SHRUG AND
SAY "IT'S A CHALLENGE", OR "I
LIKE BOATS". AND WHEN ONE OF
THE MORE FORTUNATE DECK SLOGS
(A MATE) YELLS DOWN THE HATCH —
"ALL HANDS ON DECK TO RAISE THE MAIN!" UP YOU RUN AND
HEAVE AWAY WITH A RIGHT GOOD WILL — AND SMILE —
BECAUSE YOU'RE ON DECK TO DO IT, SQUINTING IN
THE UNACCUSTOMED LIGHT. AT THE END OF
THE SUMMER, YOU'RE
PALE, EXHAUSTED,
YOUR WHOLE BEING
PERMEATED WITH
WOOD SMOKE
AND SOOT.

OU'RE SICK TO DEATH WITH THE THOUGHT OF PREPARING ANY MORE FOOD. YOU KNOW YOU'VE DONE A GOOD JOB — BUT NOT ALOFT WITH WIND AND SAIL — SPLICING LINE AND DOING SAILORLY CHORES... THAT'S MEN'S WORK! NEVER MIND. VERY FEW MEN COULD ACCOMPLISH WHAT YOU HAVE. AND WHEN YOU LOOK BACK ON IT LATER, YOU DO SO WITH WARMTH AND PRIDE AND THE REALIZATION THAT YOU SURELY WERE A VERY IMPORTANT PART OF THAT WINDJAMMER WORLD!

BOY! WHAT A GREAT SAIL! TOO BAD WE HAVE TO ANCHOR SOON.

A MOST NECESSARY PART OF LIFE ON BOARD A MAINE WINDJAMMER IS THE WOOD STOVE. THAT BIG BLACK MONSTER (OURS WAS CALLED "MAME") IS DEFINITELY NOT AN INANIMATE OBJECT. IT (OR SHE) HAS A DEFINITE PERSONALITY. TYPICALLY FEMALE, SOME DAYS SHE'S OBSTREPEROUS, CANTANKEROUS AND OBSTINATE — OTHERS WARM, WILLING AND ANXIOUS TO PLEASE. IT'S ALMOST AS IF SOMETIMES SHE HAS INDIGESTION. THAT'S PROBABLY TRUE, AS "MAME" LIKES SOME WOOD BETTER THAN OTHERS — AND BEING AN OLD BABE (YOU REALLY CAN'T CALL HER A LADY, SHE'S WORKED SO HARD ALL HER LIFE), THE WEATHER BOTHERS HER SOME — THE DAMPNESS PARTICULARLY, AND SHE'LL SMOKE AND CHOKE AND SPUTTER.

22

There's nothing more frustrating than a huge black ton of metal that has to be gotten hot enough to feed forty five ravenous people, and only green wood in the bin to burn! I decided Mame smokes too much and has a touch of emphysema. At times she needs extra air — supplied by a bellows an enterprising and sympathetic mate hooked up, with an umbilical hose wired to copper tubing that runs into the end of the fire box. The bellows became "Jeremiah" and squats under the stove like a blue bullfrog. Some foggy mornings the rhythm of pumping Jeremiah is the tempo to sing to, while Mame's breath wheezes in and out, and the flames gasp for air.

23

HEN INDEED, COOKIE IS A VERITABLE ONE-ARMED
PAPER HANGER — PUMPING, MIXING, COOKING
AND KIBITZING ALL AT THE SAME TIME.

SATURDAY AFTERNOONS DOZENS OF MILK CRATES FULL OF
DRY (WE HOPE) WOOD ARE LOADED INTO THE BILGE AREA
BEHIND THE CENTER COMPANIONWAY LADDER. FROM THERE
THE WOOD IS CARRIED THREE TIMES A DAY TO FILL
THE BOX CLOSE TO MAME'S SIDE. IF A FEW BIRCH
PIECES ARE LEFT ON TOP IN THE EVENING, THE FIVE
A.M. "BRAVE RISER" WILL HAVE THOSE GOOD STARTERS
TO USE WITH THE KINDLING. SOME COOKS RISE A LITTLE
LATER AND USE KEROSENE FOR A QUICK HOT FIRE, BUT
IT'S NOT THE SAME! BIRCH, ASH, OAK, FIR — — WHO
WOULD GIVE UP THIS FRAGRANCE ON THE EARLY MORNING
AIR FOR THAT OF KEROSENE? AND ONE OF THE BENEFITS

OF BEING

"FIRE-STARTER"

IS THE

FEEL

AND SMELL OF DAWN OUT AT ANCHOR IN THE ISLANDS —
AND THE RARE MOMENT OF BEING ALONE ON DECK. HARK,
ALL YOU OF THE GREAT TECHNICAL AGE OF MICROWAVE,
WHO SET YOUR TIMERS TO HEAT UP PLASTIC-WRAPPED
T.V. DINNERS — YOU'RE MISSING SOMETHING!

A WOOD STOVE
IS PERSONAL!
GIVEN LOVING
ATTENTION, SHE'LL
REWARD YOU WITH
THE CRUNCHIEST BREAD AND PIE CRUSTS YOU'VE EVER TASTED —
THE TENDEREST MUFFINS AND CAKES — THE MOST SUC-
CULENT MEATS. THE HEAVY IRON DOES IT, IN THE SAME
MANNER OF A CAST-IRON SKILLET OR DUTCH OVEN. YOU
MUST ATTEND TO DRAUGHTS AND VENTS. LEAVE 'EM OPEN
UNTIL SHE'S ROARING — SHOVE IN THE LEVER LETTING THE
HOT AIR CIRCULATE AROUND THE OVEN AND NOT UP THE
PIPE. CLOSE DOWN THE AIR INTO THE ASHES CHAMBER
SO YOU WON'T BE SMOKED OUT. CLOSE IT ALL DOWN TO
A SLOW-BURNING GLOW. IN OTHER WORDS, BANK IT,
AND GO AHEAD AND BAKE, BABY!

25

ALL THIS VARIES WITH DRY WEATHER OR FOG — WINDY
OR NOT — SAILING OR ANCHORED — HEELED OVER OR LEVEL.
MAME IS A GOOD FRIEND, BUT IF YOU'RE PRE-OCCUPIED,
SHE MIGHT PLAY TRICKS ON YOU. HALFWAY THROUGH THE
WEEK YOU FIND SHE WON'T DRAW, WON'T GET REALLY
HOT, SMOKES LIKE A HARLOT AND SEEMS PARTICULARLY
CRANKY (MAKING YOU THE SAME) — YOU MAY FIND SHE
HAS AN INDISPOSITION AND NEEDS CLEANING OUT. ASHES
DO PILE UP! AFTERWARDS SHE SEEMS TO
PURR AND
SETTLE
RIGHT DOWN.
IT IS A CHALLENGE.
AND BAKING — IF YOU
THINK YOU CAN SLIDE YOUR
CAKE IN THE OVEN, DUST YOUR
HANDS AND THAT'S THAT — WRONG AGAIN! THE HOTTEST
SPOT IS NEXT TO THE FIRE BOX ON THE TOP SHELF. WHEN
THAT CAKE BROWNS, IT MUST BE TURNED, THEN MOVED
AWAY FROM THE HOT SPOT AND FINISHED UP ON THE
LOWER SHELF TO BROWN THE BOTTOM.

26

No HEAT INDICATOR OR TIMER CAN HELP YOU HERE. YOU FEEL THE TEMPERATURE AND DEVELOP A GUT SENSE ABOUT IT. I SUPPOSE THAT'S WHY IT'S A SATISFACTION NEVER FELT WITH AN ELECTRIC OR GAS STOVE — THOSE COLD AND PRISTINE WHITE ENAMEL MACHINES DESIGNED BY TECHNICIANS WHO HAVE FORGOTTEN THAT WARMTH IS IMPORTANT TO THE HUMAN HEART. WHITE ENAMEL IS EASILY WIPED CLEAN, BUT HOW SWEET IT IS TO RUB STOVE BLACK INTO THE OLD GIRL AND POLISH HER UP TO A SATINY WARM SILVERY BLACK TONE. THE WARMING RACKS OVER MAME ARE A PERFECT PLACE FOR BREAD AND ROLLS TO RISE ... TO WARM PLATTERS AND SERVING DISHES AND TO KEEP ALL KINDS OF THINGS HOT WHEN MEALTIME IS NEAR AND THE TOP OF THE STOVE IS OVERFLOWING. THERE ARE LINES SLUNG BEHIND MAME WHERE WET DISH TOWELS (AND SOCKS) MAY DRY... WET SHOES GO UNDERNEATH.

27

SEA RAILS RUN AROUND THE EDGE OF THE RANGE TOP.

WHEN SAILING THEY'RE A BLESSING AND CORRAL THE

POTS WHICH HAVE A TENDENCY TO JUMP ABOUT WHEN

THE WEATHER IS LIVELY. KETTLES ARE KEPT FULL AND

HOT FOR COFFEE, TEA OR COCOA. BETWEEN MEALS

PEOPLE CAN HELP THEMSELVES. IF IT'S COOL OUT, MAME

IS MOST POPULAR. SO IS HEATHCLIFF.

HE'S MAME'S CONSTANT BUDDY AND

IS ALWAYS

BY HER

SIDE.

HE'S A

BRIGHT

RED WATER TANK AND HAS PIPES

INTO MAME'S FIRE BOX. WHEN

SHE'S HOT, SHE WARMS HEATHCLIFF'S

WATER. THERE'S A LONG HOSE RUNNING FROM

HEATHCLIFF WHICH LETS HOT WATER INTO THE SINKS

FOR WASHING UP THE MULTITUDE OF DISHES AND POTS

AND PANS. UNSCREW THE VALVE AND LET HER RIP!

SIMPLE, AND SO IMPORTANT TO GALLEY LIFE.

HEATHCLIF IS GRAVITY-FED FROM A WATER (OR "DAY") TANK ON DECK AS ARE THE GALLEY SINKS ... A GOOD WAY TO KEEP TRACK OF AMOUNTS OF WATER USED.

"WHERE'S THE BELL HOP?"

SUNDAY IS "IN PORT" DAY. PASSENGERS COME ABOARD SUNDAY AFTERNOON (TO BE READY TO SAIL MONDAY MORNING) AND TWO CREW MEMBERS HAVE "THE DUTY". ON "ADVENTURE", THERE ARE THREE MATES WHO WORK ON DECK, AND THREE GALS IN THE GALLEY (COOK, ASSISTANT COOK AND MESS GIRL). KENNY WAS FIRST MATE, AL SECOND AND PETER THIRD. COUNTING CAPT. JIM, "ADVENTURE" CARRIES SEVEN CREW. 121 FT. IS A LOT OF SHIP TO SAIL, AND PASSENGERS ARE ENCOURAGED TO HELP WITH THE FUN OF SAILING AND RUNNING THE VESSEL. THIS PARTICULAR YEAR, DEE WAS COOK, BETH ASSISTANT COOK AND PAT MESS GIRL.

WHEN PASSENGERS COME ON BOARD FOR THE FIRST TIME, THEY'RE SHOWN THROUGH THE SHIP FROM STEM TO STERN AND TOLD SOME OF THE BASIC FACTS IMPORTANT TO WIND-JAMMER LIFE. THEY'RE NOT SHOWN THE ACCOMMODATION FARTHEST FORWARD, WHERE TWO OF THE GALLEY CREW BUNK.

30

It's a small cuddy like a shoe box. The girls who occupy it have quite an exercise through the summer in getting along. There's a hatch overhead for easy access and ventilation, but by

"OH, HEH – PARDON ME, GIRLY"!

INDENTURE

summer's end those two know every detail of the other's living habits.

Passengers are shown the mess room toward the bow (seventeen fishermen had bunks here in the "olden days"). The old steps are still under the risers on the forward companionway, worn down by years of boots trampling up and down! The mess room has four long tables and there's space for everyone to eat together at one sitting. The bulkheads are mellow rubbed wood, and brass kerosene lanterns hang from the beams.

31

THE GALLEY IS NEXT WITH
MAME RULING SUPREME.
ABOVE THE MAPLE CHOPPING
BLOCK, THIRTY DOZEN EGGS
ARE STACKED AND IT'S A
LITTLE SHOCKING TO KNOW THAT THEY'RE THE SUPPLY FOR
FIVE DAYS ! FOLKS MAY COME FOR DRINKING
WATER TO THE OLD FASHIONED BRASS
COUNTRY-STYLE PUMP. WASH BASINS
FOUND IN THE STATEROOMS ARE
FILLED FROM THE OAKEN BARRELS
ON DECK. TIN DIPPERS ARE HUNG
CLOSE AT HAND.

"To pump is to flush,
It makes the waters rush
You've gotta' get up early
to avoid the morning crush!"

THE TOILETS (OR HEADS) ARE IN THE PASSAGEWAY AND EVERYONE IS GIVEN A COMPLETE DEMONSTRATION — WHICH LEVERS TO PUSH AND PULL AND HOW MANY TIMES TO PUMP, ETC. PROPER OPERATION IS IMPORTANT AS THE HEADS ARE MOUNTED BELOW THE WATERLINE AND IF A VALVE IS LEFT OPEN AND THE HEAD FLOODS — WHY IT COULD GET SLOPPY! AND, ALWAYS LOCK THE DOOR FOLKS, SO YOU WON'T BE SURPRISED.

"Hey, Al — I think we have a problem."

SOME SHIPS HAVE INSTALLED HOUSE TYPE HEADS ON DECK... A LOSS OF SHIP'S TRADITION, BUT MUCH SIMPLER. MANY HEAD JOKES DEVELOP THROUGH THE SUMMER AND THE MATES BECOME PROFICIENT AT FIXING MINOR BREAK DOWNS.

33

WASH BASINS, DRINKING GLASSES, SOAP, TOWELS AND BEDDING ARE SUPPLIED IN EACH CABIN. A FEW SHIPS HAVE SINKS IN THE STATEROOMS (ANOTHER MODERN CONCESSION) BUT MOST STILL HAVE THE OAK BARRELS ON DECK.

AN EXPLANATION IS GIVEN ABOUT USING LIGHTS AND WATER WITH CARE. SINCE THE MAJORITY OF THE SHIPS RUN UNDER SAIL ALONE, THEY HAVE NO AUXILIARY GENER- ATORS AND BATTERIES ARE CHARGED UP ON THE WEEK- ENDS WHEN IN PORT. THIS CHARGE IS SUFFICIENT FOR ELECTRIC LIGHTS DURING THE WEEK.

FOR USE WHEN NEEDED, THE SHIPS CARRY A STURDY YAWL BOAT WITH AN INBOARD DIESEL ENGINE. THIS IS USUALLY HUNG FROM DAVITS ON THE STERN. POWERFUL AND EFFICIENT, THEY'RE USED IN CALMS TO PUSH OR PULL THE "MOTHER" SHIP.

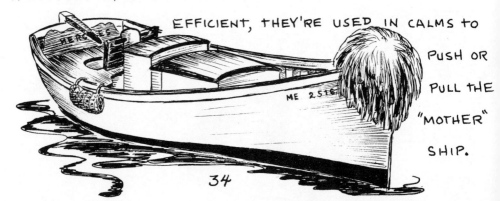

34

These perky-looking work craft have tousled fenders on the bow for protection. They may also be used for entering and leaving tight little harbors and pushing up rivers.

Quiet time on board is eleven P.M. and passengers are asked not to bring portable radios, although musical instruments are encouraged. Cabin accommodations fill the center part of the ship (the old fish hold) and cabins sleep two or four. On "Adventure" there's an after cabin with a small wood stove and many a cozy musical evening is spent there.

THE REST OF THE CREW AND THE CAPT. HAVE THEIR BUNKS IN THIS AREA . . . LIKE PULLMANS BEHIND THE SETEES. THESE ARE SHIPPY, HOMEY BUNKS, BUT IT'S RARELY QUIET UNTIL AFTER ELEVEN P.M. AND IT CAN BE A SHOCK TO OPEN YOUR EYES AND FIND SOMEONE WITH HIS NOSE SIX INCHES FROM YOURS, PEERING CURIOUSLY IN. MEALS ARE ANNOUNCED BY RINGING THE SHIP'S BELL AND THE FIRST MEAL SERVED WILL BE MONDAY BREAKFAST. TOPSIDES, THERE'S SO MUCH DECK SPACE, SHE SEEMS A MILE LONG — THERE'S NEVER A CROWDED FEELING. TO BE CLOSER TO THE ELEMENTS, SOME TAKE SLEEPING BAGS ON DECK AT NIGHT. OTHERS ENJOY THE SNUG FEELING OF THEIR BUNK BELOW.

36

$\mathcal{T}$HESE SHIPS ARE LARGE AND SAIL IN PENOBSCOT BAY'S PROTECTED WATERS, SO SEASICKNESS IS NEVER A PROBLEM.

$\mathcal{B}$ESIDES THE YAWL BOAT, "ADVENTURE" CARRIES ON THE SIDE DECK THE "SPASTIC SPIDER". THIS IS A SEINE BOAT WITH BANKS OF OARS AND SO NAMED BECAUSE OF THE OBVIOUS LOOK SHE HAS WITH SEVERAL NOVICE ROWERS FLAILING AWAY. THE "SPASTIC SPIDER" IS UTILIZED EVENINGS FOR JAUNTS ASHORE.

$\mathcal{A}$LSO ON DECK IS AN ICE BOX FOR PASSENGERS' USE AND BEER, SODAS, WINE OR OTHER GOODIES MAY BE KEPT THERE.

$\mathcal{M}$ONDAY MORNINGS ARE HECTIC. AT FIVE THIRTY A.M. "MAME" IS FIRED UP. BETH AND PAT ARE BOTH UP WHEN THE SUPPLIES COME AT SIX. THE MATES ARE ON HAND ALSO TO HELP BRING STORES ON BOARD. FRESH FRUITS AND VEGETABLES ARRIVE, AS WELL AS THE FRESH FISH.

NOUGH CAN'T BE SAID ABOUT THE EFFICIENCY AND
COOPERATION OF THE MAINE MERCHANTS WHO WORK
EXTRA HOURS ON BEHALF OF THE SHIPS, AND WHO
CARE ENOUGH TO CONSISTENTLY SUPPLY TOP QUALITY FRESH
PRODUCE, FISH, MEAT AND EGGS. SOMETIMES THERE'S A
LOT OF LAST MINUTE RUNNING AROUND TO LOCATE
SPECIALTY ITEMS — ALL DONE WITH A RIGHT GOOD WILL.

HELLO BELOW
-GROCERIES!
-OOPS!

IN BETWEEN AND AROUND STOWING GROCERIES, BREAKFAST
MUST BE PUT TOGETHER, SERVED AND PREPARATIONS MADE
FOR LUNCH AS WELL. A PANCAKE MIX IS USED THIS MORNING,
TO WHICH FRESH MAINE BLUEBERRIES ARE ADDED.

38

THREE PANS OF SAUSAGE ARE POPPED INTO THE OVEN.
THEY MUST BE SHIFTED AROUND TO BROWN. GREASE
IS POURED OFF INTO EMPTY COFFEE CANS AND PLACED
IN A SNUG CORNER UNDER THE SINK. WHEN THE
SAUSAGE IS READY AND OVER THE STOVE ON THE
WARMING RACKS, BROWNIES OR BAR COOKIES ARE
PUT IN TO BAKE (FOR LUNCH). BISCUITS OR CORNBREAD
ARE MIXED AND READY TO FOLLOW (ALSO FOR LUNCH).
EXTRA BISCUITS ARE BAKED TO SAVE FOR THE STRAW-
BERRY SHORTCAKE WHICH WILL BE DESSERT FOR DINNER.
THE BIG GRIDDLE SLIDES INTO PLACE OVER THE HOTTEST
PART OF MAME AND PILES OF HOTCAKES ARE BAKED.
AT THE SAME TIME, BETH AND PAT
ARE STOWING AWAY THE FRESH
PRODUCE IN THE BILGE
AREA IN THE MESS
ROOM. IT STAYS
COOL THERE — THE
SAME TEMPERATURE
AS THE SEA.

I'M SURE WE STOWED SOME
SPINACH IN HERE SOMEWHERE!

Emmet, our irreplaceable grocer, comes down to see if everything is O.K. and if we need anything else. You pass him your list for next week. Passengers are peering in and down the hatch, making remarks, offering help and generally adding to the confusion. They don't know quite what to expect and are a little "up" — it's sailing day! The ice comes down into the middle of everything — 500 lb. and the big ice chest must be loaded after that, preferably in the order the food will be needed during the week.

The neighboring ship rings it's bell and folks start to file in, thinking it's ours. "Ye Gods"! says Pat. The syrup has to be heated and the tables set, then we're ready. Thirty-seven hungry, enthusiastic and curious passengers pour in to find seats. The girls save the near table for the crew, who are always a bit late — and the show is on the road!

HERE'S THE FISH!

40

CAPT. JIM GIVES A SPEECH AS BREAKFAST ENDS. HE TELLS
    TIME OF DEPARTURE, WHICH DEPENDS ON THE TIDE FOR
"ADVENTURE" AS SHE'S A DEEP DRAUGHT VESSEL – ALMOST
THIRTEEN FEET BELOW THE WATER. DECK SHOES ARE
A MUST AND ARE AVAILABLE IN TOWN; PAY THE CAPT.
IN THE AFTER CABIN IF YOU HAVEN'T ALREADY. PAT
GIVES A SPEECH TOO – INTRODUCING US
AND ASSURING PEOPLE THAT THEY'RE
WELCOME IN THE GALLEY AT ANY
TIME. THERE ARE ENOUGH PAN-
CAKES FOR A FEW LOCAL FRIENDS
WHO DROP BY FOR A BITE, AND ANYONE WHO
HAS AN ERRAND TO RUN UP TOWN HAD BETTER DO
IT NOW!

DOING DISHES ON A WINDJAMMER IS FUN!

HELP IS ENLISTED FOR DISHES DUTY. POTATOES
AND ONIONS ARE PEELED AND SALT PORK IS
STARTED IN THE HUGE SOUP POT FOR
THE BEST FISH CHOWDER IN THE
        WORLD!

41

$\mathcal{T}$HE BIG MOMENT ARRIVES ! —

FORWARD LINES ARE CAST OFF, THE YAWL
BOAT ("HERCULES") ROARS AND PULLS THE BOW AROUND,
HAULING AGAINST ONE STERN LINE LEFT ASHORE UNTIL
THE SHIP IS HEADED IN THE RIGHT DIRECTION. THE PATH OF
WATER WIDENS BETWEEN THE SCHOONER AND THE
WHARF.   SOON THERE'S ENOUGH MOMENTUM AND THE
BOW IS THREADING THROUGH THE MYRIAD OF SMALL
CRAFT ANCHORED IN THE BAY. "HERCULES" LEAVES
THE BOW AND MOVES TO THE STERN TO PUSH,
CHAFFING GEAR TIGHT AGAINST THE TRANSOM.

$\mathbf{T}$HE GALLEY CREW TRIES TO BE ON DECK TO WATCH
THE LEAVE-TAKING. WHEN OUTSIDE CAMDEN HARBOR,
THE CRY COMES, "ALL HANDS
ON DECK TO RAISE THE MAIN,"
AND THE PATTERN IS ESTAB-
LISHED FOR THE WEEK. THE
MATES EXPLAIN THE "PEAK"
AND "THROAT" HALYARDS AND

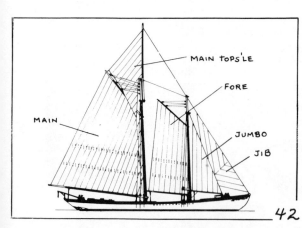

MAIN TOPS'LE

FORE

MAIN

JUMBO

JIB

*T*HIS FIRST DAY, ALMOST EVERYONE LINES UP. TO GIVE A HAND. (THE THROAT'S HEAVIEST, BUT THE PEAK TAKES LONGER!) AFTER THE HUGE MAIN IS SET, THE FORE IS RAISED. THEN UP GOES THE JUMBO AND LAST OF ALL THE JIB. AND, OF COURSE, "HERCULES" HAS TO BE HAULED UP IN THE STERN DAVITS. THE SCHOONER PAYS OFF, GATHERS HEADWAY AND — "WE'RE SAILING"! MIRACULOUSLY, IT'S ALSO TIME FOR LUNCH.

*M*ONDAY LUNCH IS ALWAYS FISH CHOWDER — HADDOCK, IF WE CAN GET IT. WHAT GOES WITH? WHY, OYSTER AND PILOT CRACKERS,

...WOODEN BOWLS WITH RED KERCHIEFS FOLDED OVER HOT BISCUITS, CELERY AND CARROT STICKS HEAPED UP WITH BLACK OLIVES FOR CONTRAST — ALWAYS THE PEANUT BUTTER TUB AND JELLY; A RACK OF MUGS FOR COFFEE — PITCHERS OF FRUIT DRINK AND ICED TEA — A HUGE BOWL OF FRESH FRUIT — APPLES, ORANGES, PEACHES, PLUMS, GRAPES, CHERRIES AND BANANAS, AND DON'T FORGET THOSE BROWNIES. ALL THIS MAGNIFICENCE IS SET OUT BELOW AND A LINE OF PASSENGERS IS FORMED FROM THE COMPANIONWAY TO THE CABIN TOP. ALL THE FOOD IS PASSED ALONG AND READY TO SERVE IN A FEW MINUTES. WE ALWAYS HAVE LUNCH ON DECK— WEATHER PERMITTING. A BUCKET OF SOAPY WATER AND A HAND MOP ARE PLACED BY THE BREAK IN THE DECK WITH DISH RACKS AND A GARBAGE PAIL, SO PASSEN-

GERS CAN WET-

MOP THEIR PLATES AND MUGS AND STACK THEM. THIS
MAKES THE CLEANUP JOB BELOW FAR EASIER WHILE
UNDER WAY.

THERE ARE, EACH TRIP, SOME "HEROES" TO US
IN THE GALLEY . . . PEOPLE WHO SHOW UP ALL
THE TIME TO HELP WASH AND DRY THE VOLUMES OF
DISHES NECESSARY TO FEED SO MANY. AFTER EVERY
MEAL, THE WOOD BOX BY THE STOVE IS STACKED AND
THE FLOOR SWEPT BEFORE THE MESS GIRL IS FINISHED.
AFTER THE EVENING'S MEAL, THE DECK BELOW IN THE
MESS ROOM AND GALLEY IS SWABBED. LEFTOVER SNACKS
ARE ON THE GALLEY COUNTER OR A TABLE IN THE MESS
ROOM ALONG WITH A BOWL OF FRUIT. 
THE WIND AND SAILING SEEM TO FOSTER
CONTINUOUS APPETITES.

THERE'S TIME ON DECK AFTER
LUNCH FOR VISITING, RELAXING
OR SAILING. GALLEY CREW MAY
CLIMB ALOFT AND THAT'S THE
PLACE TO GET COMPLETELY
AWAY.

THREE-THIRTY IS WITCHING HOUR WHEN THE GIRLS AND I
GET TOGETHER FOR PREPARATION OF THE EVENING MEAL.
MONDAY NIGHT IS EITHER ROAST TURKEY OR CHICKEN,
STUFFING, CORN ON THE COB, MAYBE CRANBERRIES, PEAS
AND MUSHROOMS, SALAD AND STRAWBERRY SHORTCAKE
(FRESH BERRIES AND REAL WHIPPING CREAM). THE VEGE-
TABLES VARY DEPENDING ON WHAT'S "IN", AS DOES THE
TYPE STUFFING AND THE WAY TO PREPARE THE BIRD.
INGENUITY BECOMES IMPORTANT. PASSENGERS WOULDN'T
KNOW THE DIFFERENCE, BUT IT'S DEADLY DULL FOR THE
CREW TO HAVE EXACTLY THE SAME FARE EVERY WEEK ALL
SUMMER. IT GETS TO BE A GAME TO HAVE VARIETY AND
INTEREST, AND ALWAYS WITH A VIEW TO EYE APPEAL AND
NUTRITIONAL BALANCE. WE SPROUT MUNG BEANS AND
ALFALFA SEEDS AND WHEAT BERRIES — USE WHEAT GERM
AND WHOLE GRAIN FLOURS FOR OUR BREADS. WE MAKE OUR

OWN GRANOLA AND
YOGURT. IF ONE OF US
WANTS TO TRY
SOMETHING NEW,
GO TO IT!

THERE'S A GOOD-NATURED RIVALRY THAT GOES ON BETWEEN THE WINDJAMMERS, AND ANY NIGHT AN ANCHORAGE MIGHT BE SHARED WITH ANOTHER SHIP. THERE MAY BE SOME VISITING BACK AND FORTH OR A COMMUNAL SONG FEST. THEN THERE'S THE CHANCE TO ROW ASHORE WITH THE "SPASTIC SPIDER" AND EXPLORE A RURAL VILLAGE OR THE COUNTRYSIDE (OR OFFSHORE LOBSTER TOWN)

— MAYBE SOME BEACHCOMBING IS TO YOUR LIKING, AND A CHANCE TO WALK OFF THE EFFECTS OF DINNER. MOST EVENINGS HAVE A MUSICAL ENDING IN THE AFTER CABIN— SHARED SEA CHANTYS OR FOLK SONGS IN THE GLOW OF KEROSENE LAMPS OR FIRELIGHT. AND FORWARD IN THE MESS ROOM, THE CLEARED TABLES ARE NOW USED FOR PLAYING CARDS, WRITING UP THE DAY'S ADVENTURES OR POST CARDS TO MAIL AT THE NEXT STOP. OR, HOW ABOUT A SNACK OF LEFT-OVER SHORTCAKE OR A BISCUIT?

Early mornings are special. It's so quiet on board. It's a good time for the cook to get her head together on menus for the day, to savor the smoke rising from the Charlie Noble (smoke stack to you land lubbers) - peaceful harbor impressions before the confusion of the day. As soon as the kettles boil, there's someone who is ready for coffee (besides you). Put the bacon on — you must fry seven lbs. Mix up muffins and break three flats of eggs (ninety!) into the largest bowl. Seasoning depends on whim. Scrambled eggs are the usual, but in an infinite variety of ways. Beth comes yawning in at six thirty and at seven Pat appears with her cheery smile to take the first coffee tray up on deck.

48

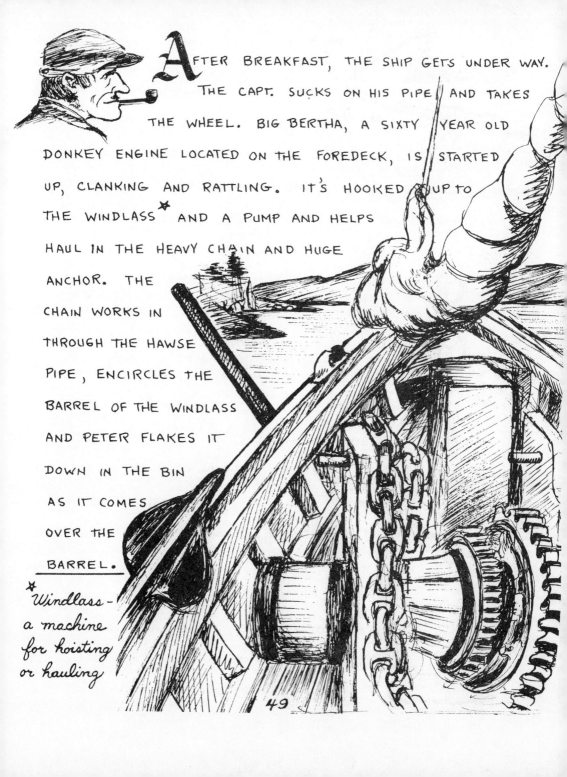

AFTER BREAKFAST, THE SHIP GETS UNDER WAY. THE CAPT. SUCKS ON HIS PIPE AND TAKES THE WHEEL. BIG BERTHA, A SIXTY YEAR OLD DONKEY ENGINE LOCATED ON THE FOREDECK, IS STARTED UP, CLANKING AND RATTLING. IT'S HOOKED UP TO THE WINDLASS* AND A PUMP AND HELPS HAUL IN THE HEAVY CHAIN AND HUGE ANCHOR. THE CHAIN WORKS IN THROUGH THE HAWSE PIPE, ENCIRCLES THE BARREL OF THE WINDLASS AND PETER FLAKES IT DOWN IN THE BIN AS IT COMES OVER THE BARREL.

*Windlass -
a machine
for hoisting
or hauling

49

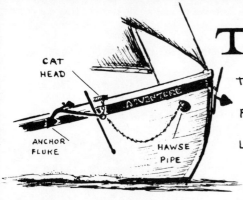

CAT HEAD

ANCHOR FLUKE

ADVENTURE

HAWSE PIPE

Two passengers pump water up through a fire hose to rinse mud from the chain and anchor. A long line with a hook at the end is dropped over the bow and hooked into a ring on the anchor. With a block and tackle, it takes three men to haul the anchor to the rail. Tucked into the bulwarks is a long handled wooden paddle called a "fluke spade". One of the mates inserts this between the anchor's fluke and the ship's hull to keep the paint from being gouged. The chain is slacked as the anchor is brought back to the cat head. The flukes are hauled up to the rail and lashed down tightly to a cleat. In the meantime, with Capt. Jim shouting directions, Kenny and Al have organized the job of raising the sails and we move away from the anchorage.

50

If that's not possible because of wind, tide, or a tight cove, the yawl boat is put to use. We sail most of the day. Folks are trying hard to get a tan, but a good share of the time it's too cool. The saying "if you don't like Maine weather, wait a minute" is based on fact. You're apt to have hot sun, rain and cool fog too — a bathing suit one minute, and a sweater the next.

Tuesday lunch is a big hot pot of some kind with crusty bread, salad and cookies. If it's "right", Beth and Pat take on deck a variety of fruits and melons. Passengers join in to chop it all up and pile it in the watermelon shells. Mighty pretty, and tastes even better! Tuesday evening dinner might be roast lamb and pilaf, vegetable, homemade bread, salad and cake or cobbler. By now folks have stopped being concerned about whether or not there will be enough food — there always is!

51

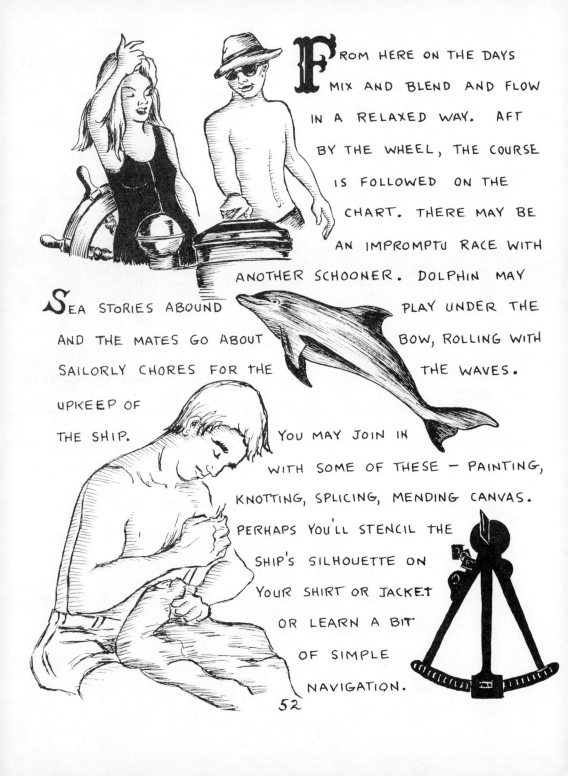

FROM HERE ON THE DAYS MIX AND BLEND AND FLOW IN A RELAXED WAY. AFT BY THE WHEEL, THE COURSE IS FOLLOWED ON THE CHART. THERE MAY BE AN IMPROMPTU RACE WITH ANOTHER SCHOONER. DOLPHIN MAY PLAY UNDER THE BOW, ROLLING WITH THE WAVES.

SEA STORIES ABOUND AND THE MATES GO ABOUT SAILORLY CHORES FOR THE UPKEEP OF THE SHIP. YOU MAY JOIN IN WITH SOME OF THESE — PAINTING, KNOTTING, SPLICING, MENDING CANVAS. PERHAPS YOU'LL STENCIL THE SHIP'S SILHOUETTE ON YOUR SHIRT OR JACKET OR LEARN A BIT OF SIMPLE NAVIGATION.

52

YOU MIGHT PLOT THE COURSE OR TAKE A SIGHT.
WHATEVER YOUR PLEASURE OR WHIM OF THE
MOMENT — DO IT! BED DOWN IN A COIL OF LINE
FOR A NAP, OR PAINT A WATERCOLOR OF A
FOG-SHROUDED ISLAND.

SPECIAL THINGS COME ALONG TO MAKE
THE TRIP UNFORGETTABLE. LOBSTER BAKE
IS ONE! L.B.! ALL WEEK EVERYONE LOOKS FORWARD TO
L.B. DAY. GASTRONOMICALLY IT'S A HIGHLIGHT (IF YOU'RE A
LOBSTER-LOVER). PASSENGERS LIKE IT, BOTH FOR THE
FOOD AND THE PICNIC AIR OF THE FIRE ASHORE. THE
GALLEY CREW LOVE IT AS THE WORK IS ALL DONE BEFORE
GOING ASHORE... SORTA LIKE A NIGHT OFF. THE ONLY
ONE WITH MIXED FEELINGS IS CAPT. JIM WHO HAS THE
BURDEN OF PICKING THE RIGHT WEATHER, THE RIGHT
DAY, AND THE RIGHT ISLAND. HE TRIES TO FIND A
SMALL ISOLATED SPOT
NOT ALREADY TAKEN BY
ANY OF THE OTHER NUMEROUS
WINDJAMMERS TRYING
TO DO THE SAME THING.

53

THERE ARE SEVERAL PLACES THROUGHOUT PENOBSCOT BAY WHERE LOBSTERS MAY BE PURCHASED EARLY IN THE DAY. THE CRITTERS ARE STASHED ON DECK IN THEIR CRATE, COVERED WITH CANVAS, DROOLED AND SQUEALED OVER, AND DOUSED REGULARLY WITH SALT WATER TO KEEP 'EM FRESH. THERE'S AN AIR OF EXCITEMENT WHEN THE BIG SHIP ANCHORS. EVERYONE GATHERS GEAR TO TAKE ASHORE — AN EXTRA SWEATER OR WINDBREAK, HIKING SHOES OR BOOTS, BAGS FOR COLLECTING AND BEACH COMBING, BUG REPELLANT, CAMERAS. THE FIRST PEOPLE IN THE "SPASTIC SPIDER" ARE THOSE WHO'VE OPTED TO HELP GATHER WOOD FOR THE FIRE. THEY TAKE THE BIG GALVANIZED TUB THAT'S THE COOKPOT. THE SECOND LOAD BRINGS THE GALLEY CREW AND MANY CRATES WITH THE PICNIC GOODIES.

*t*HE GANG ASHORE HAVE SPREAD OUT HUNTING DRIFTWOOD FOR THE MATE WHO'S STARTED THE FIRE. THERE'S A SALTY TANG IN THE AIR! GRANITE ROCKS AND GRAVEL BEACHES ...PINEY WOODS, WILD ROSES AND BERRIES...MINGLED ODORS! SNACKS ARE SPREAD OUT FOR ALL TO MUNCH. BATCHES OF RAW VEGETABLES AND DIPS – CRACKERS AND CHIPS. THERE'S A LARGE WISCONSIN CHEESE WHEEL ON THE MAPLE BOARD AND A TUB OF LEMONADE HANDY—PEANUT BUTTER AND JELLY, NATURALLY. COFFEE CANS PILED WITH BUTTER ARE PUSHED CLOSE TO THE FIRE TO MELT. THE FIRE ROARS, THE SEA WATER IN THE TUB BOILS AND THE GUYS HAND IN THE FIRST BATCH OF CRITTERS. THEY'RE HEAPED OVER WITH SEA WEED – THUS THEY STEAM (15-20 MINUTES) FOR THE BEST FLAVOR IN THE WORLD! THE TUB IS LIFTED AND DUMPED ONTO A DARK GREEN BED OF WEED. BRIGHT RED, STEAMING AND FRAGRANT!

55

CAMERAS CLICK — A SIGHT TO INSPIRE AND REMEMBER.

COME AND GET 'EM! THERE'S DRAWN BUTTER AND WHITE

WINE, PLUS SALADS AND SNACKS.

To CONQUER SIR LOBSTER:

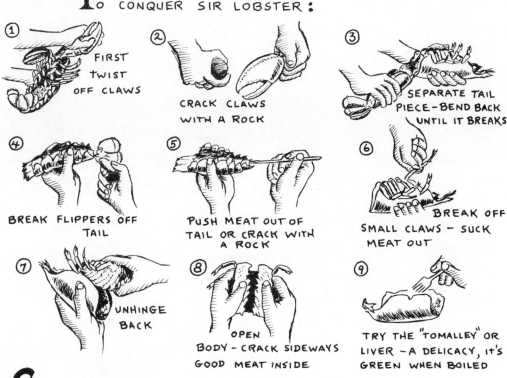

① FIRST TWIST OFF CLAWS

② CRACK CLAWS WITH A ROCK

③ SEPARATE TAIL PIECE — BEND BACK UNTIL IT BREAKS

④ BREAK FLIPPERS OFF TAIL

⑤ PUSH MEAT OUT OF TAIL OR CRACK WITH A ROCK

⑥ BREAK OFF SMALL CLAWS — SUCK MEAT OUT

⑦ UNHINGE BACK

⑧ OPEN BODY — CRACK SIDEWAYS GOOD MEAT INSIDE

⑨ TRY THE "TOMALLEY" OR LIVER — A DELICACY, IT'S GREEN WHEN BOILED

Sit ON A ROCK AND WATCH THE SUNSET AS YOU SAVOR THE

EXPERIENCE. THE LAST BATCH IS STEAMING AND READY —

SECONDS, ANYONE? THE CAPT. HOLLERS "THERE'S HOT DOGS

HERE FOR THOSE WITH MORE SENSE THAN TO EAT THOSE

THINGS!" ONCE IN A WHILE THE TIDE AND BEACH ARE RIGHT

FOR CLAMMING AND A LAYER OF CLAMS IS STEAMED IN THE
WEED WITH THE CRITTERS. THEY'RE SWEET AND SUCCULENT
TO SIP RIGHT FROM THE SHELL. TO THE GALLEY, L.B.
DAY ALSO MEANS PIE, SO THE HOMEMADE BERRY OR APPLE
PIE IS LAID OUT. BY THE FIRE ARE MARSH-
MALLOWS, AND GRAHAM CRACKERS FOR
S'MORES (SHADES OF SCOUTING). CAPT.
JIM BOILS UP HIS FAMOUS SAILORS'
COFFEE AND STIRS IT WITH A
SALTY STICK. — STRONGER THAN LOVE
AND BLACKER THAN SIN — SOMEHOW JUST RIGHT!

THE WOOD IS PILED HIGH; TIME TO SING OR STARE DREAMS
INTO THE FLAMES. A FEAST FIT FOR KINGS! THERE'S A
FEELING OF CONTENTMENT. YOU'RE REPLETE; FIRE, WIND
AND SUN BURNED AND READY TO ROW HOME TO THE LOVELY
SCHOONER SILHOUETTED IN THE DUSK.

SOMEHOW IN JUST THESE FEW
DAYS, YOU FORGET TIME
AND. LIVE FOR THE
MOMENT.

I CAN'T FIND THE ROAST BEEF!

FOR THE COOK, THE AMOUNT OF FOOD STEADILY DIMISHES IN THE ICEBOX, THE BILGE AND IN LOCKERS. WE BAKE JUICY, TENDER HAM AND SIMMER THE BEAN POTS FOR HOURS ON THE BACK OF THE STOVE. THE SMELL OF PIES AND BREAD BAKING PERMEATES THE SHIP AND IT ALL CULMINATES IN FRIDAY NIGHT'S "LAST SUPPER" WITH A TREMENDOUS ROAST BEEF WITH ALL THE TRIMMINGS AND THE PIÈCE DE RÉSISTANCE OF —

Homemade Ice Cream! IN MY MIND'S EYE, IT EVOKES MEMORIES OF GRANDPA'S FARM, HOT LAZY SUMMER DAYS, CHEWING GRASS (POT? WE'D NEVER HEARD OF IT!), WALKING ON THE RAILROAD TRACKS, WILLOW WHISTLES, TIN DIPPERS OF ICY WATER FROM THE WELL AND THE BEST ICE CREAM YOU EVER REMEMBER TASTING IN YOUR LIFE.

HERE ON THE SCHOONERS YOU'LL FIND THE SAME KIND OF FREEZERS...OLD WOODEN BUCKETS; THE METAL CANS AND THE DASHERS WITH THE WOODEN BLADES. THEY'RE PULLED OUT OF THE BILGE ON FRIDAY AFTERNOONS AND BETH RUNS

AROUND WHIPPING UP ENTHUSIASM FOR THE JOB — AND JOB
IT IS! OLD CANVAS IS PLACED ON DECK AND CHUNKS OF
ICE ARE WRAPPED AND BEATEN UNTIL CRUSHED. IT
TAKES QUITE A LOT FOR THE TWO EIGHT QUART FREEZERS.
AFTER THE CANNISTERS
WITH THE ICE CREAM MIX-
TURE ARE FITTED INTO
THE FREEZERS, LIDS
SECURED AND CRANKS
BOLTED ON, CRUSHED
ICE AND ROCK SALT
ARE SPRINKLED ALTER-
NATELY INTO THE SPACE

A WEIGHTY
AFFAIR!

AROUND THE CANS. READY! A VOLUNTEER (PREFERABLY HEAVY)
SITS ON A CUSHION ON TOP OF THE MACHINE AND TURNS ARE TAKEN
CRANKING. SLOW AND STEADY FOR THE LONG HAUL. WHEN THE
HANDLE IS BEASTLY HARD TO TURN, THE ICE CREAM IS DONE.
ADDITIONAL SALT AND ICE ARE ADDED DURING THE PROCESS.
WITH LOTS OF WILLING HANDS, IT'S EASILY ACCOMPLISHED. THE
TOPS ARE OPENED AND THE DASHERS REMOVED AND SCRAPED
(WATCH OUT YOU DON'T GET SALT IN THE ICE CREAM).
59

eVERYONE WANTS
A TASTE. THE CRANKING TAKES ABOUT THIRTY MINUTES
AND MAKES THE SMOOTHEST ICE CREAM IF IT IS ALLOWED
TO "RIPEN" AN HOUR OR TWO. IT'S WRAPPED IN THE
CANVAS AND LEFT UNTIL AFTER DINNER. AND I KNOW
NOW WHY THIS ICE CREAM IS EVERY BIT AS GOOD AS
GRANDMA'S. IT'S ALL THOSE EGGS, WHOLE MILK
AND WHIPPING CREAM. DIETETIC IT AIN'T, BUT IT
SHO' IS GOOD! WE MAKE ONE CAN OF VANILLA AND
ONE SOME OTHER FLAVOR. KINDS WE'VE MADE:
STRAWBERRY, BANANA, MAPLE NUT, COFFEE, CHOCO-
LATE, RASPBERRY, LEMON CREAM, CHERRY, JAMOCCA
NUT, BLUEBERRY, PEPPERMINT, PEACH. AND TO TOP IT
OFF, WE PUT UP A TRAY WITH CHOCOLATE SYRUP, BUTTER-
SCOTCH SAUCE, BERRIES, NUTS AND CHERRIES. MMMMMM!

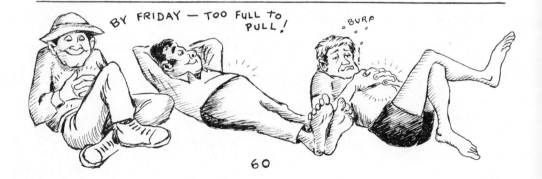

BY FRIDAY — TOO FULL TO PULL!

BURP

60

62

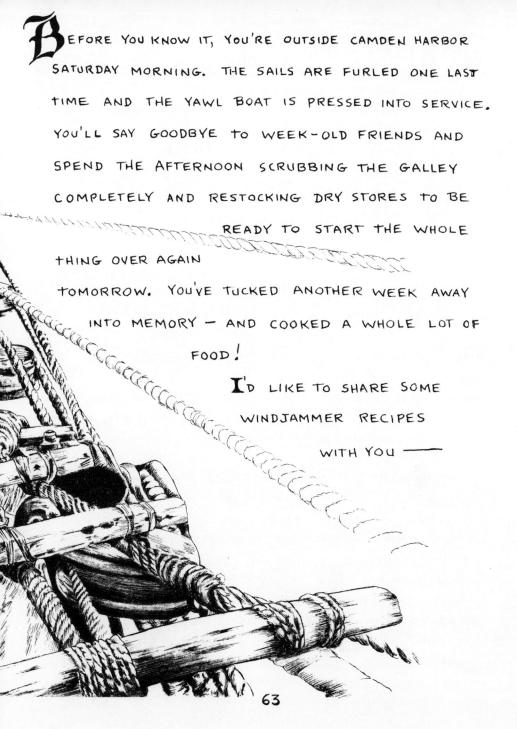

Before you know it, you're outside Camden Harbor Saturday morning. The sails are furled one last time and the yawl boat is pressed into service. You'll say goodbye to week-old friends and spend the afternoon scrubbing the galley completely and restocking dry stores to be ready to start the whole thing over again tomorrow. You've tucked another week away into memory — and cooked a whole lot of food!

I'd like to share some windjammer recipes with you ———

63

APPETIZERS

dips *snacks*

RAW VEGETABLE DIPS

#1

1 c MAYONNAISE	1/2 c WHIPPED CREAM
2 tsp. LEMON JUICE	1/4 tsp. SALT
1/2 c CHOPPED PARSLEY	1/8 tsp. PEPPER
1 TBLSP. GRATED ONION	1/4 tsp. PAPRIKA
2 TBLSP. CHOPPED CHIVES	1/4 tsp. CURRY PWD.
DASH WORCESTERSHIRE	1 MINCED CLOVE GARLIC

MIX ALL TOGETHER AND CHILL FOR A COUPLE OF HOURS.

#2

1 c MAYONNAISE	2 tsp. HORSERADISH
1 1/2 c CHILI SAUCE	2 tsp. MUSTARD SEED
1 SMALL GRATED ONION	TABASCO TO TASTE

MIX ALL TOGETHER AND CHILL UNTIL SERVING TIME. SOUR
CREAM MAY BE USED IN PLACE OF THE MAYONNAISE.

↑ ↑ ↑ ↑ ↑ ↑ ↑

SERVE EITHER OF THESE DIPS WITH STRIPS OF RAW CARROT,
GREEN PEPPER, CELERY, CAULIFLOWER, ZUCCHINI, TURNIP,
CUCUMBER, RADISHES OR MUSHROOMS.

FOR CRACKERS OR CHIPS (RAW VEGETABLES TOO!):

SPINACH DIP

1 c CHOPPED, COOKED SPINACH (WELL DRAINED) - RAW SPINACH MAY BE USED
1 c MAYONNAISE, CREAM CHEESE, SOUR CREAM OR PLAIN YOGURT

1 tsp. SEASON-ALL	1 tsp. LEMON JUICE
1 CHOPPED GREEN ONION	1 tsp. HORSERADISH

MIX ALL TOGETHER. YOU MIGHT WISH TO ADD CRUMBLED
BACON OR CHOPPED RED PIMIENTO. TO SERVE, SPRINKLE
THE TOP WITH PAPRIKA OR DECORATE WITH STRIPS OF RED
PIMIENTO.

64

SUNSHINE DIP

8 OZ. CREAM CHEESE	1/2 C MAYONNAISE
2 tSP. FINELY CHOPPED ONION	2 CLOVES GARLIC, PRESSED
1/2 C CHOPPED PARSLEY	DASH PEPPER
2 tSP. ANCHOVY PASTE	1 HARDBOILED EGG (PUT YOLK ASIDE AND CHOP WHITE FINE)

MIX ALL THE INGREDIENTS TOGETHER AND DRESS THE TOP WITH THE CRUMBLED OR SEIVED YOLK.

CALIFORNIA DIP

ALWAYS POPULAR, AND SO EASY:
1 ENVELOPE LIPTON'S DRY ONION SOUP   2 C SOUR CREAM
YOU MAY VARY THIS DIP BY ADDING CRUMBLED BLUE CHEESE, CHOPPED SEAFOOD, OR CHOPPED PIMIENTO. GARNISH WITH PAPRIKA OR CHOPPED PARSLEY.

RED HOT DIP

2 C SOUR CREAM   1 ENVELOPE SPATINI SPAGHETTI SAUCE MIX
MIX TOGETHER AND SPRINKLE THE TOP WITH CHOPPED PARSLEY.

SHRIMP DIP

1 8 OZ. PKG. CREAM CHEESE	1 CAN SHRIMP (DRAINED)
1 CAN CAMPBELLS CR. OF SHRIMP SOUP	2 tSP. LEMON JUICE
1/8 tSP. GARLIC PWD.	PAPRIKA

MIX ALL TOGETHER AND SPRINKLE THE TOP WITH PAPRIKA.

HAM DIP OR SPREAD

2 C GROUND HAM OR LUNCHEON MEAT (FINE BLADE)

1 - 8 OZ. PKG. CREAM CHEESE	1 TBLSP. MUSTARD
1 C MAYONNAISE OR SOUR CREAM	1/4 C SWEET PICKLE
1 TBLSP. FINELY CHOPPED ONION	RELISH

MIX ALL TOGETHER AND GARNISH WITH CHOPPED PARSLEY.

LOBSTER OR CRAB DIP

1 C CHOPPED LOBSTER OR CRAB MEAT

1 - 8 OZ. PKG. CREAM CHEESE   1 TSP. MUSTARD

1 TBLSP. SEASON-ALL   1 TBLSP. PWD. SUGAR

1/4 TSP. GARLIC SALT   2 TBLSP. DRY WHITE WINE

1/2 C MAYONNAISE   1 TBLSP. MINCED ONION

MIX ALL TOGETHER. HEAT IN THE TOP OF A DOUBLE BOILER. STIR
UNTIL SMOOTH. SERVE HOT OR COLD WITH CRACKERS OR CHIPS.

CLAM DIP

2 CANS MINCED CLAMS   1 - 8 OZ. PKG. CREAM CHEESE

1/2 C MAYONNAISE   1/2 TSP. DRY MUSTARD

1/4 C CHOPPED GREEN PEPPER   2 TSP. LEMON JUICE

1/4 TSP. SALT   DASH PEPPER

2 TSP. CHOPPED CHIVES   DASH TABASCO

DRAIN CLAMS AND SAVE LIQUID TO ADD LATER FOR PROPER DIPPING
CONSISTENCY. MIX ALL INGREDIENTS. TOP WITH PAPRIKA OR PARSLEY.

CLAM POT

MINCE AND SIMMER IN 1/4 LB. BUTTER:

1 MEDIUM ONION, CHOPPED   1 CHOPPED GREEN PEPPER

1 MASHED CLOVE GARLIC   1 TSP. MINCED PARSLEY

ADD: DASH TABASCO

1 TSP. OREGANO   1 TSP. LEMON JUICE

DASH CAYENNE   2 CANS MINCED CLAMS, UNDRAINED

SIMMER 5 MINUTES. ADD 1/2 C DRY BREAD CRUMBS. PLACE
MIXTURE IN A BUTTERED 9" SQUARE PAN. TOP WITH GRATED
SWISS OR AMERICAN CHEESE AND SPRINKLE WITH PARMESAN
CHEESE. BAKE AT 350° FOR 30 MINUTES. SERVE HOT OR
COLD WITH CRACKERS. - YOU MAY USE 2 C FRESH CHOPPED
CLAMS IN PLACE OF THE CANNED.

SEVICHE

USE ANY RAW FIRM WHITE FISH, CUT IN 1/2" PIECES.
COVER WITH LEMON JUICE AND REFRIGERATE FOR AT
LEAST THREE HOURS. (FISH WILL BECOME OPAQUE). DRAIN
THE LEMON JUICE AND ADD (FOR EACH CUP OF FISH) 2 TBLSP.
FINELY CHOPPED ONION, 2 TBLSP. FINELY CHOPPED GREEN
PEPPER, 1/4 C CHOPPED TOMATOES, DASH TABASCO, AND
SALT AND PEPPER TO TASTE. CHOPPED PARSLEY, CELERY
OR CUCUMBER MAY ALSO BE ADDED IF YOU WISH.

PICKLED FISH

LAYER LEFTOVER COOKED FISH IN AN EARTHENWARE
CASSEROLE WITH THINLY SLICED ONIONS (RED ONIONS ARE
ESPECIALLY NICE). MIX AND HEAT: 3/4 C WINE VINEGAR,
1/4 C WATER, 1 TBLSP. OLIVE OIL, JUICE OF 1 LEMON, 1
MINCED CLOVE GARLIC, 1 CRUSHED BAY LEAF, 6 PEPPER-
CORNS, 1 TSP. SALT, 1 CHOPPED SPRIG OF PARSLEY, AND
1/4 TSP. THYME. POUR OVER FISH AND REFRIGERATE.

SNACK NOTES

★ BREADS ★

SOUR MILK PANCAKES (FOR 4)

BEAT TWO EGGS WELL. ADD 2 C SOUR MILK (WHOLE OR CANNED MILK MAY BE SOURED WITH VINEGAR OR LEMON JUICE). MIX TOGETHER 2 C FLOUR, 2 TSP. BAKING PWD., 1 TSP. BAKING SODA, AND 1/4 TSP. SALT. FOLD INTO EGG-MILK MIXTURE. ADD 6 TBLSP. MELTED BUTTER. BEAT WELL AND BAKE ON A HOT GRIDDLE.

BUCKWHEAT CAKES (FOR 6)

COMBINE 2 C BUCKWHEAT FLOUR WITH 1 C WHITE FLOUR, 3 TBLSP. SUGAR, AND 2 TSP. SALT. CRUMBLE 1 YEAST CAKE INTO 1/2 C WARM WATER. WHEN DISSOLVED, ADD 2 C WARM MILK AND 1/4 C MELTED BUTTER. STIR LIQUID INTO DRY MIX AND BEAT UNTIL SMOOTH. COVER AND LET RISE OVERNIGHT. IN THE MORNING, STIR IN 1/2 TSP. SODA THAT'S BEEN DISSOLVED IN 1 TBLSP. WATER, AND ONE BEATEN EGG. BAKE ON A HOT GRIDDLE.

CORN GRIDDLECAKES (FOR 4)

1/2 C CORNMEAL	3/4 TSP. BAKING SODA
1 1/2 C BOILING WATER	1/3 C SUGAR
1 1/4 C SOUR MILK	1 TSP. SALT
2 C FLOUR	1 EGG, BEATEN
1 TSP. BAKING PWD.	4 TBLSP. MELTED BUTTER

ADD CORNMEAL TO BOILING WATER AND COOK FIVE MINUTES. TURN INTO A BOWL. ADD MILK AND DRY INGREDIENTS THAT HAVE BEEN MIXED AND SIFTED. ADD EGG AND BUTTER. BAKE ON A HOT GRIDDLE.

OATMEAL PANCAKES (FOR 4)

MIX TOGETHER 1 1/2 C REGULAR ROLLED OATS AND 2 C
SOUR MILK. *let set for 10 min.* BEAT IN 1 C FLOUR, 1 TBLSP. SUGAR, 1 TSP.
BAKING SODA, 1 TSP. SALT AND 2 BEATEN EGGS. ADD 1/4 C
MELTED BUTTER. BAKE ON A HOT GRIDDLE. *Sour milk 1 tbsp. lemon juice*

BISCUITS (MAKES 16)

<u>SIFT</u>: 2 C FLOUR, 3 TSP. BAKING PWD., 1 TSP. SALT.
<u>DROP IN</u>: 6 TBLSP. SHORTENING AND CUT IN WITH A
PASTRY BLENDER UNTIL THE DOUGH IS LIKE COARSE MEAL.
<u>MEASURE</u>: 3/4 C MILK. MAKE A WELL IN THE CENTER OF
THE FLOUR MIX AND POUR IN 1/2 C MILK. WORK WITH A
FORK UNTIL THE DOUGH CLINGS IN A BALL. ADD MORE
MILK IF NEEDED. <u>DROP</u> BY TBLSP. ON A BUTTERED
COOKIE SHEET, OR TURN OUT ON A FLOURED BOARD AND
ROLL OUT 1/2" THICK. DIP IN BUTTER AND PLACE ON SHEET.
<u>BAKE</u> AT 425° UNTIL BROWN (12-15 MINUTES).

VARIATIONS: <u>CHEESE</u> - ADD 1/2 C GRATED CHEESE TO THE FLOUR.
<u>ORANGE</u> <u>OR</u> <u>LEMON</u> - ADD 1 TBLSP. GRATED ORANGE OR LEMON RIND.
<u>HERB</u> - ADD 1 TBLSP. MIXED HERBS TO THE FLOUR.
<u>SEED</u> - ADD 1 TBLSP. CARAWAY, SESAME, POPPY OR DILL SEED.
<u>NUT</u> - ADD 1/2 C ANY CHOPPED NUTS.
<u>BUTTERMILK</u> - USE BUTTERMILK INSTEAD OF SWEET MILK AND ADD
2 TSP. BAKING SODA TO FLOUR.
<u>WHEAT</u> <u>OR</u> <u>GRAHAM</u> - SUBSTITUTE 1 C WHEAT OR GRAHAM FLOUR FOR
1 CUP WHITE.

FOR <u>SHORTCAKE</u> <u>DESSERT</u> - CUT IN 2 EXTRA TBLSP. BUTTER
AND ADD 1/2 C SUGAR TO THE DRY INGREDIENTS.

PLAIN MUFFINS (MAKES ABOUT 10)

2 C FLOUR   3 TBLSP. SUGAR
1 TBLSP. BAKING PWD.   1/2 TSP. SALT
1 EGG   1/4 C MELTED BUTTER
1 C MILK

SIFT DRY INGREDIENTS. MAKE A WELL IN THE CENTER. BEAT
EGG AND ADD TO BUTTER AND MILK. POUR ALL AT ONCE INTO
THE FLOUR WELL. STIR JUST ENOUGH TO MOISTEN. LINE MUFFIN
TINS WITH CUP LINERS OR GREASE WELL. FILL CUPS 2/3 FULL.
BAKE IN A 425° OVEN ABOUT 25 MINUTES.

VARIATIONS AND ADDITIONS:

1/2 C FINE CUT DATES   1/2 C RAISINS OR CURRANTS
1/2 C FINE CUT APRICOTS   1/2 C FINE CUT PRUNES
1/2 C CHOPPED PEACHES   1/2 C CHOPPED APPLE
1/2 C CHOPPED NUTMEATS   1/2 C MASHED PUMPKIN
1/2 C MASHED BANANA   SPICES TO DRY INGREDIENTS
1/2 C WELL-DRAINED CRUSHED PINEAPPLE
6 SLICES COOKED, CRUMBLED BACON

BLUEBERRY OR CRANBERRY MUFFINS — USE "PLAIN MUFFIN" RECIPE,
BUT INCREASE SUGAR TO 1/3 C AND FOLD INTO THE BATTER BEFORE
THE DRY INGREDIENTS ARE COMPLETELY MOIST — 1 C FRESH
BERRIES (LIGHTLY FLOURED) OR 1 CUP CHOPPED CRANBERRIES
(WITH 1 TSP. GRATED ORANGE OR LEMON RIND).

TRY DIPPING THE TOPS OF HOT MUFFINS IN MELTED BUTTER - THEN CINNAMON-SUGAR.

BRAN MUFFINS (1 GALLON)

2 C - 100% NABISCO BRAN
2 C - BOILING WATER — POUR ON BRAN — ALLOW TO COOL.

2 1/3 C SUGAR ⎫ CREAM OIL TO
1 C OIL   ⎬ SUGAR AND ADD 1 EGG AT A
4 EGGS   ⎭ TIME, BEATING AFTER EACH

1 QT SOUR MILK — ADD TO CREAMED MIX AND BEAT WELL.

70

SIFT TOGETHER : 5 C FLOUR, 5 TSP. SODA , 1 1/2 TSP. SALT.
ADD — 4 C KELLOGS' ALL BRAN
FOLD — INTO MOIST MIXTURE.
ADD — 1 C RAISINS IF DESIRED.
STORE IN A COVERED CONTAINER IN REFRIGERATOR.
USE AS NEEDED. DIP OUT — DO NOT STIR. BAKE AT 375°
20 MINUTES OR UNTIL DONE.

OATMEAL MUFFINS (MAKES 12 MEDIUM)

1 C ROLLED OATS	1 C SOUR MILK
1 C FLOUR	1/2 TSP. SALT
1/2 TSP. BAKING SODA	1 1/2 TSP. BAKING PWD.
1/2 C MELTED BUTTER	1/2 C BROWN SUGAR, PACKED
1 EGG, BEATEN	

COMBINE OATS AND SOUR MILK. SOAK 30 MINUTES. SIFT
FLOUR, SODA, SALT AND BAKING PWD. ADD BUTTER, BROWN
SUGAR AND EGG TO OATMEAL MIXTURE. BLEND. STIR IN DRY
INGREDIENTS UNTIL JUST MOISTENED. SPOON INTO GREASED
MUFFIN PANS. BAKE AT 350° — 25 MINUTES.

CORN BREAD

1 C YELLOW CORNMEAL	4 TSP. BAKING PWD.
1 C FLOUR	1 C MILK
1/4 C SUGAR	1 EGG
1 TSP. SALT	1/4 C MELTED BUTTER

COMBINE DRY INGREDIENTS. ADD MILK, EGG AND BUTTER.
POUR INTO A GREASED 8" SQUARE PAN. BAKE AT 425°
25 MINUTES OR UNTIL WELL-BROWNED.

CHEDDAR SPOON BREAD

1 CAN CR. CORN (1 LB.)	1½ C GRATED CHEDDAR CHEESE
⅓ C MELTED BUTTER	3/4 C MILK
1 C CORN MEAL	2 EGGS, BEATEN
1 TSP. SALT	½ TSP. BAKING SODA
1 CAN (4 OZ.) RED PIMIENTOS	

MIX ALL INGREDIENTS EXCEPT PIMIENTOS AND CHEESE — WET FIRST, THEN DRY. POUR HALF OF BATTER INTO A 9 X 9" SQUARE BUTTERED PAN. SPREAD WITH CHOPPED PIMIENTOS AND HALF OF CHEESE. COVER WITH THE REMAINING BATTER AND SPRINKLE WITH THE REST OF THE CHEESE. BAKE AT 400° FOR 30 - 45 MINUTES. COOL 15 MINUTES BEFORE CUTTING.

SCOTCH OATCAKES

1 C FLOUR	1 3/4 C ROLLED OATS
1 TBLSP. SUGAR	1/4 C WHEAT GERM
1 TSP. BAKING PWD.	½ TSP. SALT
⅓ C BUTTER	½ C MILK

MIX DRY INGREDIENTS AND BLEND IN MELTED BUTTER. POUR IN MILK AND MIX UNTIL STICKY. DIVIDE DOUGH INTO EIGHT BALLS AND ROLL OUT ONE AT A TIME — VERY THIN. CUT IN WEDGES (AS A PIE) AND BAKE ON GREASED COOKIE SHEETS AT 375° FOR 15 - 20 MINUTES UNTIL BROWN. THESE KEEP WELL IF COVERED TIGHTLY.

QUICK COFFEECAKE

SIFT: 2 C FLOUR, 3/4 C SUGAR, 2 TSP. BAKING PWD., ½ TSP. SALT
CUT IN: ½ C BUTTER   BREAK: 1 EGG INTO A MEASURING CUP AND FILL WITH MILK TO MAKE 1 C. BEAT AND ADD TO DRY INGREDIENTS WITH 1 TSP. VANILLA.
POUR BATTER INTO A GREASED 9 X 13" PAN. COVER WITH STREUSEL OR FRUIT TOPPING. BAKE AT 350° FOR 30 - 45 MINUTES.   72

STREUSEL TOPPING: MIX 1/2 C BROWN SUGAR, 1/4 C FLOUR, 2
   TSP. CINNAMON, 1/4 C MELTED BUTTER. SPRINKLE OVER BATTER
   BEFORE BAKING (1/2 C CHOPPED NUTS MAY BE ADDED TOO).

FRUIT TOPPING: COVER BATTER WITH A LAYER OF THIN-SLICED
   APPLES, PEACHES OR BERRIES. SPRINKLE WITH BROWN
   SUGAR (NUTS TOO, IF YOU WISH). BEAT 1 EGG WITH 1/4 C
   CREAM AND POUR ON TOP OF FRUIT. BAKE.

BUTTERMILK COFFEECAKE

2 1/4 C FLOUR	1/2 TSP. SALT
1/2 TSP. CINNAMON	1 C BROWN SUGAR, PACKED
3/4 C SUGAR	3/4 C SALAD OIL
1/2 C NUTMEATS	1 TSP. CINNAMON
1 TSP. BAKING SODA	1 TSP. BAKING PWD.
1 EGG, BEATEN	1 C BUTTERMILK

SIFT FLOUR WITH SALT AND 1/2 TSP. CINNAMON. ADD BROWN
SUGAR AND GRANULATED SUGAR AND OIL. BEAT UNTIL BLENDED
AND LIGHT. REMOVE 3/4 C AND SET ASIDE FOR TOPPING.
ADD NUTS AND 1 TSP. CINNAMON TO IT. TO REMAINING MIX
ADD SODA, BAKING PWD., EGG AND BUTTERMILK. MIX UNTIL
SMOOTH. SPOON INTO A BUTTERED 9 X 13" PAN. SPRINKLE
WITH RESERVED TOPPING. BAKE AT 350° FOR 30 MINUTES.

BANANA BRAN BREAD

BEAT: 1/4 C SOFT BUTTER WITH 1/2 C SUGAR.

ADD: 1 EGG, 1/4 C MILK AND 1 TSP. VANILLA.

STIR IN: 1 1/2 C MASHED BANANA, 1 1/4 C 40% BRAN
   CEREAL OR RAISIN BRAN AND 1/2 C CHOPPED NUTS.

SIFT TOGETHER: 1 1/2 C FLOUR, 2 TBLSP. BAKING PWD.,
   1/2 TSP. BAKING SODA, AND 1/2 TSP. SALT.

ADD AND STIR ONLY UNTIL COMBINED. PLACE IN A
WELL-GREASED 9 X 5 X 3" LOAF PAN AND BAKE AT
350° ABOUT 50 MINUTES. COOL BEFORE SLICING.

MOIST BANANA BREAD

2 LB. RIPE BANANAS
JUICE OF 1 LEMON
3/4 LB. BROWN SUGAR
3 EGGS, BEATEN
1/2 LB. SOFT BUTTER
2 TSP. BAKING PWD.

2 C FLOUR
3 WHOLE CLOVES, CRUSHED
1/2 TSP. PWD. GINGER
1/2 TSP. CINNAMON
1/2 TSP. NUTMEG
1 TSP. VANILLA

BLEND MASHED BANANAS AND LEMON JUICE UNTIL CREAMY. IN A SEPARATE BOWL, CREAM SUGAR, EGGS AND BUTTER. ADD BANANAS AND MIX UNTIL SMOOTH. SIFT TOGETHER DRY INGREDIENTS AND ADD GRADUALLY TO WET. IF BATTER IS TOO STIFF, ADD UP TO 1/4 C MILK. STIR IN VANILLA. POUR INTO A GREASED BREAD PAN AND BAKE AT 350° FOR 50-60 MINUTES OR UNTIL DONE. LET COOL IN PAN 5 MINUTES BEFORE TURNING OUT.

DATE NUT LOAF

POUR: 1 C BOILING WATER (WITH 1 TSP. BAKING SODA MIXED IN) OVER 1 - 8 OZ. PKG. PITTED DATES. LET COOL. ADD: 2 BEATEN EGGS, 3/4 C SUGAR, 1 TSP. BAKING PWD., 1/2 TSP. SALT, 2 C FLOUR AND 1/2 C CHOPPED NUTS. BAKE IN A 9" GREASED LOAF PAN IN A 350° OVEN FOR 1 HOUR.

ZUCCHINI BREAD

2 C GRATED ZUCCHINI
3 BEATEN EGGS
1 C OIL

To THESE, ADD 2 C SUGAR (OR 1/3 LESS HONEY), 3 C FLOUR, 1 TSP. BAKING SODA, 1 TSP. SALT, 1/4 TSP BAKING PWD., 3 TSP. CINNAMON, 2 TSP. VANILLA, AND 1 C CHOPPED WALNUTS.

GREASE WELL A 9" LOAF PAN AND BAKE 1 HOUR AT 350°.

74

CRANBERRY NUT BREAD

3 C FLOUR
3 TSP. BAKING PWD.
1/2 TSP. BAKING SODA
1 TSP. SALT
1/2 C BUTTER

2/3 C SUGAR
1 EGG
3/4 C MILK
1 C CRANBERRY-ORANGEPRELISH
OR - 1 C GROUND RAW CRANBERRIES

1 C CHOPPED PECANS

CREAM BUTTER AND SUGAR. ADD BEATEN EGG AND BLEND. ADD SIFTED DRY INGREDIENTS ALTERNATELY WITH MILK. STIR IN RELISH AND NUTS. POUR BATTER INTO A GREASED 9 x 5" LOAF PAN AND BAKE AT 350° ABOUT 1 HOUR OR UNTIL DONE.

WHEAT ORANGE BREAD

1 1/2 C WHOLE WHEAT FLOUR
1 1/2 C WHITE FLOUR
3/4 C SUGAR
2 TBLSP. GRATED ORANGE PEEL
2 TSP. BAKING PWD.

1/2 TSP. SALT
3/4 C ORANGE JUICE
1/2 C MILK
1/2 C OIL   1 EGG
1/2 C CHOPPED NUTS

COMBINE ALL INGREDIENTS. STIR UNTIL THE DRY PARTICLES ARE MOISTENED... ABOUT 75 STROKES. POUR INTO A GREASED 9 x 5" LOAF PAN. SPRINKLE WITH A MIXTURE OF 1 TBLSP. SUGAR AND 1/2 TSP. CINNAMON. BAKE AT 350° ONE HOUR OR UNTIL A TOOTHPICK INSERTED IN THE CENTER COMES OUT CLEAN.

OATMEAL RAISIN BREAD

2 C FLOUR
3/4 TSP. BAKING SODA
1 C ROLLED OATS
1/3 C BUTTER
1 EGG, BEATEN

2 TSP. BAKING PWD.
1 1/2 TSP. SALT
1 C RAISINS
1/3 C BROWN SUGAR
1 1/4 C BUTTERMILK

CREAM BUTTER AND SUGAR. ADD EGG AND BUTTERMILK. ADD MILK ALTERNATELY WITH COMBINED DRY INGREDIENTS. BAKE AT 350° IN A GREASED 9 x 5" LOAF PAN FOR 1 HOUR.

75

IRISH SODA BREAD

4 C FLOUR	1/8 TSP. CARDAMOM (OR CORIANDER)
1 TSP. SALT	1/4 C BUTTER
3 TSP. BAKING PWD.	1 EGG, BEATEN
1 TSP. BAKING SODA	1 3/4 C SOUR MILK
1/4 C SUGAR	

MIX FLOUR, SALT, BAKING PWD., SODA, SUGAR AND SPICE. CUT IN BUTTER WITH A PASTRY BLENDER UNTIL CRUMBLY. MIX EGG WITH SOUR MILK. ADD DRY INGREDIENTS AND STIR UNTIL BLENDED. TURN OUT ON A FLOURED BOARD AND KNEAD TWO OR THREE MINUTES. DIVIDE DOUGH IN HALF AND SHAPE EACH INTO A ROUND LOAF. PLACE IN GREASED PIE OR CAKE PAN. CUT CROSSES IN TOPS OF LOAVES. BAKE AT 375° 35-40 MINUTES.

VARIATION: OMIT CARDAMON OR CORIANDER AND ADD 2 C CURRANTS OR RAISINS TO THE FLOUR MIX WITH 1 1/4 TSP. CARAWAY SEED (OPT.)

SPICED PUMPKIN BREAD

1 1/2 C SUGAR	1/2 C RAISINS
1/2 C VEGETABLE OIL	1/2 TSP. BAKING SODA
2 EGGS, BEATEN	1/4 TSP. BAKING PWD.
1 C CANNED PUMPKIN	1 TSP. SALT
1 1/4 C FLOUR	1/2 TSP. ALLSPICE AND CLOVES
3/4 C WHEAT FLOUR	1/2 TSP. CINNAMON AND NUTMEG

MIX SUGAR AND OIL. ADD EGGS, PUMPKIN AND 1/3 C WATER AND MIX WELL. SIFT DRY INGREDIENTS TOGETHER; ADD TO PUMPKIN MIXTURE AND STIR UNTIL JUST MOISTENED. STIR IN RAISINS. POUR INTO A GREASED 9 X 5 X 3" LOAF PAN AND BAKE AT 350° FOR ONE HOUR. — A MOIST BREAD.

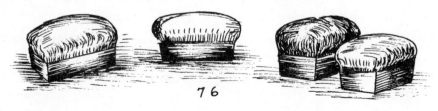

Yeast Breads

ADVENTURE BASIC BREAD (2 LOAVES)

SCALD: 2 C WHOLE MILK. ADD 1/4 LB. BUTTER AND LET IT MELT. ADD 1/2 C SUGAR. STIR UNTIL IT'S DISSOLVED AND COOL UNTIL LUKEWARM. SPRINKLE IN 3 TBLSP. DRY YEAST AND LET IT PROOF. AFTER IT FOAMS UP, ADD 1 TBLSP. SALT AND WORK IN ENOUGH FLOUR (APPROXIMATELY 8 C) TO FORM A SOFT DOUGH. TURN OUT ON A FLOURED BOARD AND KNEAD UNTIL SATINY. PLACE IN AN OILED BOWL, BRUSH THE TOP WITH BUTTER, COVER AND LET RISE AN HOUR OR UNTIL DOUBLE. KNOCK DOWN AND MAKE INTO ROLLS OR LOAVES. PLACE IN 2 GREASED BREAD PANS. LET RISE UNTIL DOUBLE AND BAKE AT 375° - 1/2 HOUR OR UNTIL BROWN AND DONE.

VARIATIONS: THIS RECIPE MAY BE MADE WITH VARIOUS TYPES OF FLOUR, BUT DON'T USE MORE THAN HALF OF A WHOLE GRAIN FLOUR LIKE WHEAT, RYE, GRAHAM — THE OTHER HALF WHITE. WHEAT GERM MAY BE ADDED, OR SEEDS AND HERBS — TRY A TBLSP. OF MILLET.

CINNAMON ROLLS: USE THE BASIC RECIPE, BUT CUT 4 TBLSP. EXTRA BUTTER INTO HALF THE FLOUR. BEAT 2 EGGS AND ADD TO LIQUID AFTER THE YEAST HAS PROOFED. AFTER THE FIRST RISING, ROLL OUT (1/4 AT A TIME) DOUGH 1/2" THICK. BRUSH WITH MELTED BUTTER, SPRINKLE WITH BROWN SUGAR AND CINNAMON (RAISINS AND NUTS IF DESIRED). ROLL UP AS FOR A JELLY ROLL. CUT 3/4" SLICES AND PLACE IN BUTTERED PANS. LET RISE UNTIL DOUBLE AND BAKE AT 375° FOR 15-20 MINUTES.

BUTTERMILK CHEESE BREAD

1 C BUTTERMILK	1 C WARM WATER
2 TBLSP. SUGAR	1/2 TSP. BAKING SODA
2 1/2 TSP. SALT	6 C FLOUR
1 TBLSP. BUTTER	1 1/2 C (6 OZ.) GRATED
2 PKG. DRY YEAST	AMERICAN CHEESE

SCALD MILK WITH SUGAR, SALT AND BUTTER. COOL. DISSOLVE
YEAST IN WARM WATER AND STIR IN COOLED MILK MIXTURE.
STIR SODA INTO 2 C FLOUR. ADD THIS TO MILK MIX AND BEAT
UNTIL SMOOTH; ADD GRATED CHEESE AND BEAT IN; ADD REST OF
FLOUR TO FORM A STIFF DOUGH. TURN OUT ON FLOURED BOARD
AND KNEAD UNTIL SATINY. TURN INTO AN OILED BOWL AND LET
RISE UNTIL DOUBLE IN BULK. PUNCH DOWN AND SHAPE INTO TWO
LOAVES. LET RISE AND BAKE AT 350° — 30 - 45 MINUTES.

CORNMEAL BRAID

2 C MILK	1/4 C WARM WATER	7 C FLOUR
6 TBLSP. SUGAR	1 PKG. DRY YEAST	CORNMEAL (FOR PANS)
1 TBLSP. SALT	2 EGGS, BEATEN	1 EGG, BEATEN
1/2 C BUTTER	1 C CORN MEAL	3 TBLSP. WATER

SCALD MILK AND STIR IN SUGAR, SALT AND BUTTER. COOL.
DISSOLVE YEAST IN WARM WATER AND ADD TO MILK. STIR IN EGGS,
CORNMEAL AND 3 1/2 C FLOUR; BEAT. ADD REMAINING FLOUR.
TURN OUT ON FLOURED BOARD AND KNEAD UNTIL SATINY. PLACE
IN OILED BOWL, COVER AND LET RISE UNTIL DOUBLE. PUNCH
DOWN AND LET DOUGH REST 10 MINUTES. DIVIDE DOUGH IN HALF
AND EACH HALF IN THIRDS. MAKE THE THIRDS INTO 12" STRIPS.
BRAID 3 STRIPS AND PLACE IN GREASED, CORNMEAL SPRINKLED
BREAD PANS. REPEAT WITH OTHER THREE STRIPS. LET RISE
UNTIL DOUBLE AND BAKE AT 350° 25 MINUTES. MIX EGG
AND WATER — BRUSH TOPS OF LOAVES AND BAKE TEN
MINUTES MORE.

ANADAMA BREAD

SPRINKLE: 1 1/4 C CORNMEAL INTO 4 1/2 C BOILING WATER.
COOL TO LUKEWARM.

ADD: 3 TBLSP. YEAST SOFTENED IN 3/4 C WARM WATER,
1 C MOLASSES, 1 1/2 TBLSP. SALT, 1/3 C OIL OR BUTTER.

ADD: 4 1/2 C WHITE FLOUR, 4 1/2 C WHEAT FLOUR

TURN: OUT ON A FLOURED BOARD AND KNEAD, ADDING
FLOUR IF NECESSARY, UNTIL SMOOTH AND SATINY.
PLACE IN AN OILED BOWL, BUTTER THE TOP OF DOUGH, COVER
AND LET RISE UNTIL DOUBLE IN BULK. PUNCH DOWN AND
SHAPE INTO LOAVES. PUT INTO GREASED BREAD PANS THAT
HAVE BEEN SPRINKLED WITH CORNMEAL (3 LOAVES). BAKE
IN A 375° OVEN 30 MINUTES OR UNTIL DONE.

ANDREA'S NEWFOUNDLAND BREAD (3 LOAVES)

2 PKG. YEAST	1 1/2 TSP. SALT
3 C WARM WATER	2 TBLSP. BUTTER
10 C FLOUR	1 C MOLASSES

PROOF YEAST IN 1 C WARM FOR TEN MINUTES. SIFT FLOUR,
SALT AND CUT IN BUTTER. MAKE A HOLE IN THE FLOUR AND
ADD DISSOLVED YEAST, MOLASSES AND 2 C WARM WATER.
MIX THOROUGHLY. KNEAD UNTIL SATINY AND LET RISE
UNTIL DOUBLE IN BULK. PUNCH DOWN, SHAPE INTO LOAVES
AND PLACE IN GREASED BREAD PANS. LET RISE UNTIL
DOUBLE AND BAKE AT 375° FOR 40-45 MINUTES. OR
MAKE ROLLS AND BAKE AT 400° FOR ABOUT 12 MINUTES.

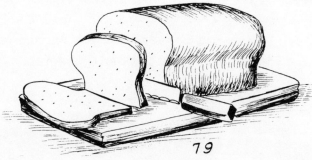

OATMEAL BREAD

MIX 2 C WARM WATER, 1/2 C HONEY AND 1 C OATMEAL. STIR IN 2 PKG. DRY YEAST AND LET PROOF. STIR IN 2 BEATEN EGGS AND 1/3 C MELTED BUTTER. ADD 1 TBLSP. SALT. MIX IN 7 TO 7 1/2 C FLOUR, IN 2 ADDITIONS. TURN OUT ON A FLOURED BOARD AND KNEAD UNTIL SMOOTH. PLACE IN A GREASED BOWL, OIL TOP, COVER AND LET RISE UNTIL DOUBLE IN BULK. PUNCH DOWN AND MAKE INTO ROLLS OR 2 LOAVES OF BREAD. PLACE IN 2 GREASED BREAD PANS, LET RISE AND BAKE AT 400° UNTIL DONE.

THE FOLLOWING BREAD HAS AN INTERESTING TASTE AND TEXTURE AND USES LEFTOVER OATMEAL IF YOU'VE COOKED TOO MUCH FOR BREAKFAST:

COOKED OATMEAL BREAD

1 1/2 C COOKED OATMEAL, WARM	1 C WARM MILK
2 PKG. DRY YEAST	1 TBLSP. SALT
1/2 C WARM WATER	1/4 C DARK BROWN SUGAR
1 TSP. SUGAR	4-5 C FLOUR

DISSOLVE YEAST AND SUGAR IN WARM WATER AND ALLOW TO PROOF. ADD MILK, SALT, BROWN SUGAR AND YEAST MIXTURE TO THE OATS AND STIR WELL, THEN STIR IN FLOUR, 1 CUP AT A TIME. TURN OUT ON A FLOURED BOARD AND KNEAD UNTIL SMOOTH, ADDING FLOUR IF NECESSARY. PLACE IN A BUTTERED BOWL AND TURN TO COAT THE DOUGH. COVER AND LET RISE UNTIL DOUBLE. PUNCH DOWN AND SHAPE INTO 2 LOAVES. PLACE IN BUTTERED 8 X 4 X 2" PANS. LET RISE UNTIL AL-MOST DOUBLE AND BAKE AT 375° 45-50 MINUTES. AFTER REMOVING FROM PANS, THE LOAVES MAY BE RETURNED TO THE OVEN FOR ABOUT 5 MINUTES FOR A FIRMER CRUST.

WHEAT GERM BREAD

2 C MILK	1/3 C MOLASSES	2 PKG. YEAST
1 1/2 C WATER	2 TBLSP. BROWN SUGAR	1/2 C WARM WATER
1 C WHEAT GERM	1 TBLSP. SALT	1 TBLSP. SUGAR
1/3 C BUTTER	3 C WHEAT FLOUR	4 C WHITE FLOUR

SCALD MILK AND WATER. PLACE WHEAT GERM, MOLASSES, SALT, SUGAR AND BUTTER IN A BOWL. POUR IN HOT MILK AND BLEND. ADD WHEAT FLOUR AND BEAT. LET COOL. DISSOLVE YEAST IN 1/2 C WARM WATER, ADD SUGAR AND STIR UNTIL DISSOLVED. ADD TO COOLED MIX. WORK IN WHITE FLOUR UNTIL YOU HAVE A SOFT DOUGH. TURN OUT ON A FLOURED BOARD, LET DOUGH REST TEN MINUTES AND THEN KNEAD UNTIL SMOOTH. PLACE IN A BUTTERED BOWL, OIL TOP, COVER AND LET RISE UNTIL DOUBLE IN BULK. KNOCK DOWN AN DIVIDE INTO 3 LOAVES. PLACE IN BUTTERED BREAD PANS, LET RISE AND BAKE AT 400° FOR TEN MINUTES AND THEN AT 325° FOR 30 MINUTES.

SPROUTED WHEAT BREAD

2 C WHEAT SPROUTS	5 C WHEAT FLOUR
1/4 C WARM WATER	1 TBLSP. SALT
1 TBLSP. HONEY	2 C WARM WATER
1 TBLSP. YEAST	3 TBLSP. OIL
1/2 C PWD. NON-FAT MILK	3 TBLSP. HONEY

SPROUT WHEAT GRAINS UNTIL THE ROOT IS AS LONG AS THE GRAIN (3 DAYS). MIX WATER, HONEY AND YEAST. LET FOAM (10 MINUTES). MIX PWD. MILK WITH FLOUR AND SALT BEFORE ADDING YEAST MIX. COMBINE WATER, OIL AND HONEY WITH SPROUTS AND STIR THE MIX INTO THE FLOUR. BEAT UNTIL THE BATTER IS SMOOTH AND ELASTIC (1 MINUTE). DROP A CUPFULL ONTO A GREASED SHEET AND LET IT SPREAD INTO A FLAT ROUND. BAKE AT 350° FOR 30 MINUTES. OR BAKE IN SMALL, GREASED LOAF PANS. THIS MAKES A HEAVY, MOIST BREAD WITH A WONDERFUL FLAVOR.

SWEDISH LIMPA BREAD

1 PKG. YEAST	2 TBLSP. MELTED BUTTER	1 TBLSP. CARAWAY SEED
1 TSP. SUGAR	1/3 C HONEY	2 TBLSP. GRATED ORANGE PEEL
1/4 C WARM WATER	2 TSP. SALT	2 1/2 C RYE FLOUR
2 C WARM BEER	1 TSP. CARDAMOM	3 C WHITE FLOUR

DISSOLVE YEAST AND SUGAR IN WATER (5 MINUTES). MIX BEER, HONEY, BUTTER AND SALT. STIR. ADD TO YEAST. ADD CARDAMOM, CARAWAY SEED AND ORANGE PEEL. MIX FLOURS AND ADD THREE CUPS TO LIQUID. BEAT. COVER AND LET RISE UNTIL DOUBLE. BEAT DOWN AND ADD ENOUGH FLOUR TO MAKE A STIFF DOUGH. TURN OUT ON A FLOURED BOARD AND KNEAD UNTIL SMOOTH. FORM INTO TWO LOAVES, PLACE IN GREASED BREAD PANS AND LET RISE UNTIL DOUBLE. BAKE AT 375° — 30-45 MINUTES.

BETH'S OLD WORLD RYE BREAD

2 C RYE FLOUR	2 TSP. SALT
1/4 C COCOA	2 TBLSP. CARAWAY SEED
2 PKG. YEAST	2 TBLSP. BUTTER
1 1/2 C WARM WATER	2 1/2 C WHITE OR
1/2 C MOLASSES	WHEAT FLOUR

COMBINE RYE FLOUR AND COCOA (UNSWEET). DISSOLVE YEAST IN 1/2 C WARM WATER. COMBINE MOLASSES, THE REMAINING WATER, SALT AND CARAWAY SEED IN LARGE BOWL. ADD RYE FLOUR MIX, YEAST, BUTTER AND 1 C WHITE OR WHEAT FLOUR. BEAT UNTIL SMOOTH. SPREAD REST OF FLOUR ON BOARD WITH DOUGH AND KNEAD IN ENOUGH TO MAKE A SMOOTH, ELASTIC DOUGH. PLACE IN AN OILED BOWL, TURN TO COAT, COVER AND LET RISE UNTIL DOUBLE. SHAPE INTO A ROUND LOAF ON A BUTTERED SHEET SPRINKLED WITH CORNMEAL. LET RISE. BAKE AT 375° FOR 35-40 MINUTES.

82

NEW ENGLAND RAISIN BREAD

MIX TOGETHER 1 1/4 C WARM MILK, 1/2 C SUGAR AND CRUMBLE IN
2 YEAST CAKES. STIR UNTIL DISSOLVED. WHEN YEAST FOAMS, ADD
1 TBLSP. SALT, 4 BEATEN EGGS, AND 1/2 C MELTED BUTTER. STIR
IN 1 BOX SEEDLESS RAISINS. MIX IN 6 1/4 - 6 3/4 C FLOUR. TURN
OUT ON A FLOURED BOARD AND KNEAD UNTIL SATINY. PLACE IN AN
OILED BOWL, TURN TO COAT DOUGH, COVER AND LET RISE. PUNCH
DOWN AND FORM INTO 2 LOAVES. LET RISE IN 9 x 5" GREASED
LOAF PANS AND BAKE AT 350° FOR 30 - 45 MINUTES.

DATE-NUT YEAST BREAD

1 PKG. YEAST	1/4 C WARM WATER
1 - 3/4 C MILK	1 C BROWN SUGAR
2 TSP. SALT	1/2 C MELTED BUTTER
2 EGGS, BEATEN	6 C FLOUR
1 C CHOPPED DATES	1/2 C CHOPPED NUTS

DISSOLVE YEAST IN WATER. SCALD MILK AND ADD BROWN SUGAR,
SALT AND BUTTER. COOL. ADD YEAST AND STIR IN EGGS. MIX DATES
AND NUTS INTO FLOUR. STIR MILK MIX INTO DRY INGREDIENTS.
LET REST TEN MINUTES, THEN TURN OUT ON A FLOURED BOARD
AND KNEAD UNTIL SMOOTH. LET RISE UNTIL DOUBLE IN BULK. KNOCK
DOWN, FORM INTO TWO LOAVES, AND BAKE AT 350° IN GREASED
BREAD PANS FOR 30 - 45 MINUTES OR UNTIL DONE.

STEPHEN TABER STEAMED BROWN BREAD

(ENOUGH BATTER FOR THREE ONE LB. COFFEE CANS)

2 C WHITE FLOUR	2 C ROLLED OATS	1 TSP. SALT
2 C CORNMEAL	2 C MOLASSES	1/4 BOX RAISINS (OPT.)

MIX 1/2 C BOILING WATER WITH 2 HEAPING TSP. BAKING SODA.
ADD 3 1/2 C WATER (AMOUNT OF LIQUID IS DOUBLE THE MEASURE OF
ANY ONE OF THE DRY INGREDIENTS). MIX ALL TOGETHER AND POUR
INTO GREASED CANS. COVER WITH FOIL AND PLACE ON RACK IN
KETTLE — 1" OF WATER IN KETTLE. COVER AND STEAM 3 HOURS.

HOMEMADE GRANOLA

WE FOUND MAKING GRANOLA A GREAT PLEASURE, AND WOULD TOSS IN WHATEVER WE WANTED TO, USING INGREDIENTS AT HAND. IT'S OFTEN A MATTER OF PERSONAL PREFERANCE. FOR GUIDELINES IN AMOUNTS OF SWEET AND OIL, YOU MAY TRY THE FOLLOWING:

4 C ROLLED OATS	1 C SUNFLOWER SEED	1/3 C SALAD OIL
1 C WHEAT GERM	1 C CHOPPED NUTS	1 TSP. VANILLA
1 C CORNMEAL	2 C ALL BRAN	1/4 C MAPLE SYRUP
1/4 C MILLET	1 TSP. CINNAMON	(OPT.)
1/2 C SESAME SEED	1/2 C HONEY	

MIX HONEY, OIL AND VANILLA AND STIR INTO DRY INGREDIENTS. BY HAND IS THE BEST WAY. COCONUT MAY BE ADDED OR POPPY SEED. SPREAD MIX IN FLAT PANS AND BAKE AT 350° ABOUT 25 MINUTES, STIRRING ONCE IN A WHILE. WHEN GOLDEN BROWN, RE-MOVE FROM OVEN AND STIR IN ANY DRIED FRUITS YOU WISH — 1 C CHOPPED DATES OR 1 C RAISINS — DRIED APPLE, APRICOTS, ETC. COOL AND STORE IN A TIGHTLY COVERED CONTAINER.

ON "ADVENTURE", CEREAL MORNING IS SO SATISFYING! WHEN THE BELL RINGS, A LARGE POT OF HOT CEREAL IS READY ON THE STOVE. IT MAY BE OATMEAL, CREAM OF WHEAT OR WHEATENA — PERHAPS IT'S A COMBINATION OF ALL THREE, WITH WHEAT GERM, BROWN SUGAR AND PWD. MILK STIRRED IN. THE TABLES HOLD PACKAGES OF DRY CEREAL, BOWLS OF OUR GRANOLA, RAISINS, BROWN SUGAR, FRESH BERRIES OR BANANAS, PITCHERS OF MILK, AND PLATTERS OF COFFEECAKE OR BUNS HOT FROM THE OVEN... ALONG WITH SLICES OF HONEYDEW OR CANTALOUPE (OR GRAPEFRUIT HALVES) ....A GREAT START FOR A MORNING IN MAINE!

BREAD NOTES

CAKES

CAKE MIXES ARE OFTEN USED ABOARD SHIP FOR AN UNEXPECTED BIRTHDAY OR IF TIME BECOMES TIGHT. THERE ARE MANY THINGS THAT CAN BE DONE TO MAKE THEM SPECIAL, FROM ADDING FLAVORED JELLO, PUDDING OR DREAM WHIP TO THE BATTER, TO USING FRUITS AND NUTS. SEE "MARLIN SPIKE CAKE" BELOW. THE GOODIE BOX OVER THE CHOPPING BLOCK IS KEPT STOCKED WITH BIRTHDAY CANDLES, FOOD DYES, AND ICING TIPS SO WE CAN HELP ANYONE CELEBRATE ANYTHING. BAKING CAKES FROM SCRATCH IS BEST. HERE ARE A FEW FAVORITES:

MARLIN SPIKE CAKE

3/4 C COLD WATER

1 - 3 OZ. PKG. LEMON JELLO

4 EGGS, BEATEN

1 PKG. YELLOW CAKE MIX

3/4 C SALAD OIL

GRATED RIND 1 LEMON

2 C CONFECTIONERS' SUGAR

JUICE OF 2 LEMONS

MIX COLD WATER WITH GELATIN. ADD EGGS, CAKE MIX, GRATED RIND AND OIL AND BEAT. POUR INTO A GREASED AND FLOURED 9 X 13" PAN AND BAKE AT 350° ABOUT 35 MINUTES OR UNTIL DONE. WHILE WARM, PUNCH HOLES ALL OVER CAKE (ABOUT 2" APART) WITH A MARLIN SPIKE. MIX LEMON JUICE AND CONFECTIONERS' SUGAR AND DRIZZLE OVER CAKE.

HUNDRED DOLLAR CAKE

2 C FLOUR

1 C SUGAR

4 TBLSP. UNSWEET COCOA

2 TSP. BAKING SODA

1 C COLD WATER

1 C MAYONNAISE

1 TSP VANILLA

PLACE ALL INGREDIENTS IN A BOWL AND BEAT WELL. BAKE AT 350° IN A GREASED, FLOURED 9" SQUARE PAN FOR ABOUT 30 MINUTES. TOP WITH "BOILED WHITE FROSTING".

86

BOILED WHITE FROSTING

BRING 1 C SUGAR AND 1/3 C WATER TO A BOIL. SIMMER
UNTIL IT SPINS A THREAD. BEAT ONE EGG WHITE UNTIL
STIFF AND SLOWLY POUR SUGAR SYRUP IN, BEATING
AS YOU POUR. THIS IS ENOUGH FOR ONE LAYER CAKE.

HOT MILK SPONGE CAKE

2 EGGS   1 C FLOUR   1 TSP. BAKING PWD.
1 C SUGAR   1/8 TSP. SALT   1/2 C BOILING MILK

BEAT EGGS THREE MINUTES. ADD SUGAR AND BEAT TWO
MINUTES. STIR IN BOILING MILK. SIFT FLOUR, SALT
AND BAKING PWD. AND FOLD IN GENTLY. POUR INTO A
GREASED 9" SQUARE PAN AND BAKE AT 325° FOR
30 MINUTES OR UNTIL DONE.

LAZY TOPPING: MIX IN A SAUCEPAN — 3 TBLSP. BUTTER,
5 TBLSP. BROWN SUGAR, 2 TBLSP. CREAM AND 1/2 C
SHREDDED COCONUT. HEAT UNTIL BUTTER MELTS. SPREAD
ON WARM CAKE AND BROIL UNTIL TOPPING BUBBLES.

POUND CAKE

SIFT: 4 C FLOUR, 1 TSP. SALT, 1/2 TSP. MACE, 4 TSP. BAKING PWD.
CREAM WELL: 1 1/2 C BUTTER AND 3 C SUGAR
ADD: 1 AT A TIME, BEATING WELL AFTER EACH — 8 EGGS
ADD: FLOUR MIX ALTERNATELY WITH 1 C MILK, 2
      TSP. VANILLA AND 2 TBLSP. BRANDY
STIR: ONLY UNTIL WELL BLENDED.
BAKE: IN TWO GREASED 9 X 9" BREAD PANS (LINED
      WITH OILED BROWN PAPER) AT 325° — 1 HR.
SEED CAKE: SAME RECIPE AS ABOVE, BUT ADD
      2 TSP. CARAWAY SEED, 1/3 C SHAVED CITRON
      AND 1 TSP. GRATED LEMON RIND.

PINEAPPLE UPSIDE DOWN CAKE

1 C BROWN SUGAR	3 EGGS
½ C BUTTER	1 ½ TSP VANILLA
1 - 20 OZ. CAN PINEAPPLE SLICES, DRAINED	2 ½ C FLOUR
MARASCHINO CHERRIES	2 ½ TSP. BAKING PWD.
1 C GRANULATED SUGAR	½ TSP. SALT
2/3 C SHORTENING	1 C MILK

IN RECTANGULAR BAKING PAN, MIX BROWN SUGAR AND BUTTER. COOK AND STIR OVER LOW HEAT UNTIL MIXTURE BUBBLES. REMOVE FROM HEAT AND ARRANGE PINEAPPLE SLICES AND CHERRIES IN THE SUGAR MIX. IN A BOWL, CREAM SHORTENING AND SUGAR UNTIL LIGHT. ADD EGGS ONE AT A TIME, BEATING WELL. ADD VANILLA. SIFT DRY INGREDIENTS AND ADD TO CREAMED MIX ALTERNATELY WITH MILK. POUR BATTER OVER FRUIT AND BAKE AT 350° FOR ABOUT 45 MINUTES. OTHER KINDS OF FRUIT CAN BE SUBSTITUTED FOR PINEAPPLE

ALMOND CAKE (MAKES 30 PIECES)

6 EGGS, SEPARATE	2 C GROUND BLANCHED ALMONDS
1 C SUGAR	1/8 TSP. SALT
½ C FLOUR	1/8 TSP. CREAM OF TARTER
1 TSP. BAKING PWD.	1 TSP. GRATED LEMON PEEL
¼ TSP. ALMOND EXT.	LEMON SYRUP

BEAT YOLKS UNTIL LIGHT. GRADUALLY BEAT IN ½ C SUGAR UNTIL THICK AND LEMON-COLORED. SIFT FLOUR WITH BAKING PWD. AND STIR IN. ADD ALMOND EXT. AND HALF OF ALMONDS. MIX ONLY UNTIL WELL DISTRIBUTED. BEAT WHITES FOAMY. ADD SALT AND CREAM OF TARTER AND BEAT UNTIL STIFF, ADDING OTHER ½ C SUGAR. FOLD IN PEEL AND REST OF ALMONDS. GENTLY FOLD YOLK MIX INTO WHITES. BAKE AT 350° IN A BUTTERED 9 X 13" PAN FOR 30 MINUTES. COOL 10 MINUTES. TURN OUT - CUT IN DIAMOND WEDGES AND POUR OVER HOT—

LEMON SYRUP: MIX IN A SAUCEPAN 3/4 C SUGAR, 3 TBLSP. LEMON JUICE AND ¼ C WATER. BOIL AND STIR UNTIL SUGAR DISSOLVES.

APPLECAKE

1/4 C MELTED BUTTER	1 C FLOUR	1/2 TSP. NUTMEG
1 C SUGAR	1 TSP. BAKING SODA	3 C GRATED APPLE
1 EGG, BEATEN	1/4 TSP. SALT	3/4 C NUTMEATS (OPT.)
1 TSP. VANILLA	1/2 TSP. CINNAMON	

CREAM BUTTER AND SUGAR AND BLEND IN EGG AND VANILLA.
SIFT DRY INGREDIENTS AND STIR IN. FOLD IN APPLES AND NUTS.
POUR INTO A GREASED 9" OVEN DISH. BAKE AT 375° ABOUT
30 MINUTES. SERVE HOT OR COLD WITH LEMON SAUCE OR
WHIPPED CREAM.

APPLESAUCE SPICE CAKE

1/2 C BUTTER	2 1/2 C FLOUR	1/2 TSP. ALLSPICE
2 C SUGAR	1/2 TSP. SALT	1 C CHOPPED RAISINS
1 EGG	1/2 TSP. CINNAMON	1/2 C CHOPPED NUTS
		2 TSP. BAKING SODA
1 1/2 C APPLESAUCE	1/2 TSP. CLOVES	1/2 C BOILING WATER

CREAM BUTTER AND SUGAR. STIR IN EGG AND APPLESAUCE. SIFT DRY
INGREDIENTS AND ADD ALTERNATELY WITH BOILING WATER (IN WHICH
THE SODA HAS BEEN DISSOLVED). STIR IN RAISINS AND NUTS. BAKE IN
A GREASED 9 X 13" PAN AT 350° FOR 30 - 45 MINUTES.

BLUEBERRY PUDDING CAKE

2 C BLUEBERRIES	1/2 TSP. NUTMEG	1 TSP. VANILLA
2 TBLSP. LEMON JUICE	3/4 C SUGAR	1 C SUGAR
1 C FLOUR	1/2 C MILK	1 TBLSP. CORNSTARCH
2 TSP. BAKING PWD.	1 EGG	1 C BOILING WATER
1/4 TSP. SALT	1/4 C MELTED BUTTER	

PLACE BLUEBERRIES AND LEMON JUICE IN AN 8 X 8" PAN. MIX FLOUR,
BAKING PWD., SALT, NUTMEG AND 3/4 C SUGAR. BEAT IN MILK, EGG,
MELTED BUTTER AND VANILLA. SPREAD OVER BERRIES. MIX 1 C
SUGAR WITH CORNSTARCH AND SPRINKLE OVER BATTER. POUR
BOILING WATER OVER ALL. BAKE AT 350° FOR 40 - 45 MINUTES.
(OTHER FRUITS MAY BE USED IN PLACE OF THE BLUEBERRIES)

89

CARROT-NUT CAKE

3 C FLOUR

2 TSP. BAKING PWD.

2 TSP. SODA — PLACE IN A BOWL AND MAKE A WELL IN THE CENTER.

3/4 TSP. SALT

ADD: 4 BEATEN EGGS, 1½ C SALAD OIL AND 2 C SUGAR. BEAT.

ADD: 2 C GRATED CARROT   ½ C RAISINS (FLOURED)

1 C CHOPPED PECANS   2 TSP. CINNAMON

POUR: INTO A BUTTERED 9 X 13" PAN AND BAKE AT 325°
ONE HOUR. SPRINKLE WITH PWD. SUGAR TO SERVE.

FRUIT COCKTAIL CAKE

2 EGGS   1½ C SUGAR   2 C FLOUR

2 C FRUIT COCKTAIL   2 TSP. BAKING SODA   1 TSP. SALT

MIX ALL TOGETHER AND POUR INTO A GREASED AND FLOURED
9 X 13" PAN. SPRINKLE ½ C BROWN SUGAR AND ½ C CHOPPED
NUTS ON TOP. BAKE AT 350° FOR 30-40 MINUTES. FROST WITH:
½ C BUTTER, ½ C CANNED MILK OR CREAM AND ¾ C WHITE
SUGAR (HEAT TOGETHER AND POUR OVER WARM CAKE).

GINGERBREAD

½ C BUTTER   1 TSP. CINNAMON   JUICE 1 ORANGE

½ C SUGAR   1 TSP. NUTMEG   RIND 1 ORANGE

1 C MOLASSES   ⅓ C BRANDY (OR COFFEE)   1 TSP. SODA

½ C MILK   3 EGGS, BEATEN   2 TBLSP. WARM WATER

1 TBLSP. GINGER   3 C FLOUR   1 C RAISINS

CREAM BUTTER AND SUGAR. ADD MOLASSES, MILK, SPICES AND
BRANDY OR COFFEE. ADD FLOUR AND EGGS ALTERNATELY TO BATTER.
STIR IN JUICE AND RIND. DISSOLVE SODA IN WARM WATER AND
ADD. BEAT UNTIL LIGHT. FOLD IN RAISINS. BAKE AT 350° IN A
GREASED 9 X 13" PAN FOR ONE HOUR. SERVE WITH WHIPPED
CREAM OR LEMON SAUCE.

CHOCOLATE CAKE

3 SQUARES BITTER CHOCOLATE

2 C FLOUR

2 C SUGAR

1 TSP. SALT

1 1/2 TSP. BAKING SODA

1/2 C SHORTENING

3/4 C MILK

3/4 TSP. BAKING PWD.

1/2 C MILK

3 EGGS, UNBEATEN

1 TSP. VANILLA

PLACE MELTED CHOCOLATE AND NEXT SIX INGREDIENTS IN A BOWL. BEAT 300 STROKES. STIR IN BAKING PWD; ADD NEXT THREE INGREDIENTS. BEAT 300 STROKES. POUR INTO A GREASED AND FLOURED 9 x 13" PAN (OR TWO 9" LAYER CAKE PANS). BAKE AT 350° FOR 30-45 MINUTES.

CHOCOLATE FROSTING

MIX 1 1/4 C SUGAR, AND 1 C EVAPORATED MILK IN A PAN. BRING TO A BOIL AND SIMMER 6 MINUTES. REMOVE FROM FIRE AND ADD 5 SQUARES BITTER CHOCOLATE. BLEND. STIR IN 1/2 C BUTTER AND 1 TSP. VANILLA. BEAT TILL THICK.

QUICK LEMON SAUCE (1 3/4 c)

MIX 1/2 C SUGAR, 1/8 TSP. SALT, AND 2 TBLSP. CORNSTARCH IN A SAUCEPAN. GRADUALLY STIR IN 1 C BOILING WATER. COOK UNTIL THICK AND CLEAR. REMOVE FROM HEAT AND STIR IN 2 TBLSP. BUTTER AND THE JUICE AND GRATINGS OF 1 LEMON. — GOOD ON APPLECAKE AND GINGERBREAD.

PUDDING OR CAKE SAUCE

HEAT 1/4 C MILK IN THE TOP OF A DOUBLE BOILER. STIR IN 1 C SUGAR AND 2 BEATEN EGG YOLKS. STIR AND COOK UNTIL THICK. REMOVE FROM FIRE AND COOL. FOLD IN STIFFLY BEATEN EGG WHITES AND FLAVOR SAUCE WITH VANILLA, BRANDY OR RUM.

91

COOKIES

SCOTCH SHORTBREAD

BEAT: 1 C BUTTER WITH 1 C SIFTED CONFECTIONERS' SUGAR. WHEN
LIGHT AND CREAMY, BEAT IN: 2 EGGS AND ¼ C SOUR CREAM. SIFT
AND STIR IN: 2½ C FLOUR, 1 TSP. BAKING PWD. YOU MAY ADD
1 TSP. GRATED LEMON RIND. PRESS DOUGH INTO FOUR 8" ROUNDS.
FLUTE THE EDGES AND PRICK DOUGH WELL. THE TOPS MAY BE
SPRINKLED WITH CHOPPED, BLANCHED ALMONDS. BAKE AT 325°
ABOUT 20 MINUTES UNTIL LIGHTLY BROWNED. CUT IN WEDGES WHILE
STILL WARM.

CINNAMON CRUNCH

1 C FLOUR	½ C SUGAR	1 EGG WHITE
¼ TSP. SALT	1 EGG YOLK	¼ C SUGAR
½ TSP. CINNAMON	2 TBLSP. MILK	¼ TSP. CINNAMON
⅓ C BUTTER	½ TSP. VANILLA	¼ C CHOPPED NUTS

SIFT FLOUR, SALT AND CINNAMON. CREAM BUTTER AND SUGAR.
STIR IN FLOUR MIX. BEAT YOLK, MILK AND VANILLA AND ADD.
SPREAD IN A BUTTERED 9 X 9" PAN. BEAT EGG WHITE SLIGHTLY
AND BRUSH ON DOUGH. MIX SUGAR, CINNAMON AND NUTS. SPRINKLE
ON DOUGH. BAKE AT 350° FOR 30 MINUTES. CUT IN SQUARES
WHILE WARM. COOL IN PAN.

SWEDISH SPICE COOKIES

1 C BUTTER	2 TSP. BAKING SODA	1½ TBLSP. GRATED
1½ C SUGAR	1 TBLSP. WARM WATER	ORANGE RIND
2 TSP. DARK SYRUP	3 C FLOUR	2 TSP. CINNAMON
1 EGG	1 TSP. GINGER	½ TSP. CLOVES

CREAM BUTTER AND SUGAR. STIR IN SYRUP AND EGG. ADD
SODA DISSOLVED IN WARM WATER. ADD THE REST OF THE
INGREDIENTS. FORM INTO A ROLL AND CHILL. SLICE AND
BAKE ON AN UNGREASED COOKIE SHEET AT 400° FOR
5 TO 10 MINUTES.

93

OATMEAL COOKIES

3/4 C SHORTENING	1 EGG	1 C FLOUR
1 C BROWN SUGAR	1/4 C WATER	1 TSP. SALT
		1/2 TSP. BAKING SODA
1/2 C GRANULATED SUGAR	1 TSP. VANILLA	3 C REGULAR OATS

BEAT SHORTENING, SUGARS, EGG, WATER AND VANILLA UNTIL CREAMY.
SIFT TOGETHER FLOUR, SALT AND SODA. ADD TO CREAMED MIX.
BLEND WELL AND STIR IN OATS. DROP BY TSP. ON A GREASED
COOKIE SHEET. BAKE AT 350° FOR 10-15 MINUTES. (FOR VARIETY,
YOU MAY ADD CHOPPED NUTS, RAISINS, CHOCOLATE CHIPS OR COCONUT.

PEANUT-BUTTER COOKIES

2 1/2 C FLOUR	1 C WHITE SUGAR	1/2 TSP. SALT
1 TSP. BAKING PWD.	2 EGGS	1 C PEANUT-BUTTER
		1 C BROWN SUGAR
1 C BUTTER	2 TSP. BAKING SODA	1 TSP. VANILLA

CREAM BUTTER AND PEANUT-BUTTER. ADD SUGARS, THEN EGGS. SIFT
DRY INGREDIENTS AND MIX IN. ADD VANILLA. CHILL DOUGH. FORM INTO
BALLS AND PUT ON GREASED BAKING SHEET. FLATTEN BALLS WITH
A FLOURED FORK. BAKE AT 375° 10-15 MINUTES.

MOLASSES COOKIES

3/4 C BUTTER	1/4 C MOLASSES	1 TSP. CINNAMON
1 C SUGAR	2 C FLOUR	1 TSP. GINGER
		1 TSP. PWD. CLOVES
1 EGG	2 TSP. BAKING SODA	1/2 TSP. SALT

MIX ALL TOGETHER AND CHILL. MAKE INTO WALNUT SIZE BALLS. ROLL
IN GRANULATED SUGAR AND BAKE AT 350° FOR 10-12 MINUTES

GRANOLA COOKIES

3/4 C SHORTENING	1 TSP. VANILLA	1 TSP. CINNAMON
1 C BROWN SUGAR	3 C GRANOLA	1/2 TSP. BAKING SODA
1/2 C GRANULATED SUGAR	(CRUSH SLIGHTLY)	1/2 TSP. PWD. CLOVES
1 EGG	1 1/4 C FLOUR	1 C RAISINS
1/4 C WATER	1 TSP. SALT	1 C NUTMEATS (OPT.)

MIX ALL INGREDIENTS TOGETHER. DROP BY TSP. ON AN UNGREASED
BAKING SHEET. BAKE AT 350° FOR 10-15 MINUTES.

SEVEN LAYER BARS

1/4 c BUTTER

1 c GRAHAM CRACKER CRUMBS

1 c SHREDDED COCONUT

1 PKG. (6 OZ.) CHOCOLATE CHIPS

1 PKG. (6 OZ) BUTTERSCOTCH CHIPS

1 CAN SWEETENED CONDENSED MILK

1 C CHOPPED NUTS

MELT BUTTER IN A 13 x 9" PAN. SPRINKLE GRAHAM CRUMBS EVENLY OVER BUTTER. PRESS DOWN. SPRINKLE ON COCONUT, THEN CHOCOLATE CHIPS AND BUTTERSCOTCH CHIPS. POUR MILK EVENLY OVER ALL. SPRINKLE NUTS ON TOP. BAKE AT 350° FOR 30 MINUTES. CUT IN 1 x 2" BARS.

BUTTERSCOTCH FRUIT BARS

1/2 TSP. BAKING PWD.

1/3 c FLOUR

1/3 c WHEAT GERM

7/8 c BROWN SUGAR

1/2 C PWD. MILK

1/4 TSP. SALT

1/2 CUBE MELTED BUTTER

1 TBLSP. MOLASSES

2 EGGS

1 TSP. VANILLA

1 TSP. ALMOND EXT.

1/2 C CHOPPED DATES

4 EACH CHOPPED DRIED

FIGS AND APRICOTS

1/2 C CHOPPED NUTS

MELT BUTTER - ADD SUGAR AND STIR. ADD EVERYTHING ELSE WITH FRUIT AND NUTS LAST. LINE 8 x 8" PAN WITH ALUMINUM FOIL. BAKE AT 350° ABOUT 30 MINUTES. CUT INTO BARS WHILE WARM.

BROWNIES

2 SQUARES BITTER CHOCOLATE

1/3 c BUTTER

1/2 TSP. BAKING PWD.

2/3 C FLOUR

1/4 TSP. SALT

2 EGGS

1 C SUGAR

1 TSP. VANILLA

1/2 C CHOPPED NUTS

BEAT EGGS WELL. BEAT IN SUGAR. MELT CHOCOLATE AND BUTTER AND ADD. BLEND IN VANILLA. SIFT FLOUR, BAKING PWD. AND SALT AND STIR INTO CHOCOLATE MIX. ADD NUTS. BAKE AT 350° IN A GREASED 8 x 8" SQUARE PAN FOR 25 MINUTES. CUT INTO 20 PIECES.

CHEWY CARAMEL BROWNIES

1 C FLOUR

2 C LT. BROWN SUGAR

1 C CHOPPED NUTS

1/2 C SHORTENING

2 EGGS

3/4 TSP. SALT

2 TSP. VANILLA

2 TSP. BAKING PWD.

BEAT ALL TOGETHER WELL. BAKE IN A GREASED COOKIE SHEET AT 350° FOR 25 MINUTES. COOL 15 MINUTES. CUT.

95

MOM'S CHOCOLATE COOKIES

2/3 C BUTTER   3/4 C MILK   2 1/2 C FLOUR
1 1/2 C SUGAR   3/4 C BITTER COCOA 1 C CHOPPED NUTS
                                          3/4 TSP. SALT
2 EGGS   3 TSP. BAKING PWD.   1 1/2 TSP. VANILLA

CREAM BUTTER AND SUGAR. ADD EGGS AND MILK. SIFT COCOA WITH
REST OF DRY INGREDIENTS. STIR INTO BATTER. ADD NUTS AND VANILLA.
DROP BY TSP. ON GREASED COOKIE SHEET. BAKE AT 400° ABOUT TEN
MINUTES. COOL AND FROST WITH: 2 TBLSP. MELTED BUTTER, 1/4 C
COCOA, 4 TBLSP. HOT WATER AND 1 TSP. VANILLA. USE ENOUGH PWD.
SUGAR TO THICKEN. (MIX OVER HOT WATER).

COOKIE NOTES

MISCELLANEOUS DESSERTS ★

<u>PUDDINGS, PUDDINGS, PUDDINGS</u> —

So MANY THINGS MAY BE DONE WITH INSTANT OR COOKED PUDDING MIXES. THEY'RE A BLESSING. USE YOUR IMAGINATION TO ENHANCE THEM.   AFTER YOUR PUDDING IS PREPARED, FOLD IN WHIPPED CREAM, DREAM OR COOL WHIP, OR TRY SOME OF THE FOLLOWING ADDITIONS:

<u>VANILLA</u>
1. MANDARIN ORANGES WITH GRATED ORANGE PEEL.
2. DRAINED CRUSHED PINEAPPLE (TRY FLAVORING IT MINT).
3. LAYER WITH CANNED PIE FILLING - TOP WITH TOASTED ALMONDS.
4. SOAK DRIED DATES AND/OR FIGS IN ORANGE JUICE AND STIR IN WITH CHOPPED WALNUTS.
5. FOLD IN BANANAS — SEASON WITH SHERRY, RUM OR BRANDY.
6. FOLD IN SHAVED CHOCOLATE OR CHOCOLATE CHIPS.
7. LAYER OR RIBBON WITH ICE CREAM SAUCES.
8. DECORATE WITH COCONUT, CRUSHED GRANOLA, CHOPPED NUTS, NUTMEG, CHERRIES, SHAVED CHOCOLATE — WHATEVER !

<u>BUTTERSCOTCH</u>
1. FOLD IN CRUSHED PEANUT BRITTLE
2. CHOCOLATE CHIPS AND/OR NUTS OR COCONUT
3. DISSOLVE STRONG INSTANT COFFEE AND ADD WHEN MIXING.
4. PRALINE - SPRINKLE CHOPPED PEANUTS ON TOP.

<u>CHOCOLATE</u>
1. FOLD IN BANANAS AND WHIPPED CREAM.
2. FOLD IN CRUSHED PEPPERMINT CANDY.
3. FOLD IN CHOPPED NUTS, COCONUT OR MINIATURE MARSHMALLOWS.

COOKED PIE SHELLS MAY BE FILLED WITH ANY PUDDING COMBINATION.

MAINE CRAZY PUDDING

1 1/4 C SUGAR
5 TBLSP. BUTTER } CREAM TOGETHER

ADD: 2 1/2 C FLOUR
2 1/2 TSP. BAKING PWD.   1 1/4 TSP. SALT
2 1/2 TSP. BAKING SODA   1 1/4 TSP. NUTMEG
ALTERNATELY WITH 1 1/4 C MILK.   ADD 1 C RAISINS

SAUCE: 2 1/2 C BROWN SUGAR   OR DATES
5 TBLSP. BUTTER
5 C BOILING WATER   AND 5 TBLSP. LEMON JUICE.
POUR OVER PUDDING IN A LARGE RECTANGULAR PAN
(GREASED). BAKE AT 375° - 1 HOUR. SERVE WARM
WITH WHIPPED CREAM.

FLUFFY BREAD PUDDING

SOAK FOR 15 MINUTES: 4 C DICED FRESH BREAD
(3 1/2 IF STALE) OR CAKE — IN 3 C WARM MILK (OR
2 C MILK AND 1 C FRUIT JUICE) AND 1/4 TSP. SALT.
COMBINE AND BEAT WELL: 3 EGG YOLKS
1/2 C SUGAR, 1 TSP. VANILLA AND 1/2 TSP. NUTMEG.
ADD: GRATED RIND AND JUICE 1/2 LEMON (1/4 C
RAISINS, DATES OR NUTS OR 1/2 C DRAINED
CRUSHED PINEAPPLE OR 1/4 C ORANGE MARMALADE.)
POUR: THESE INGREDIENTS OVER SOAKED BREAD.
STIR LIGHTLY UNTIL BLENDED.
BEAT: 3 EGG WHITES UNTIL STIFF AND FOLD IN.
BAKE IN A BUTTERED DISH SET IN A PAN OF
HOT WATER — ABOUT 45 MINUTES AT 350°.
TOP WITH CREAM OR DABS OF A TART JELLY,
OR BOTH.

98

SURPRISE APPLESAUCE PUDDING

2 C GRAHAM CRACKER CRUMBS

2 TBLSP. MELTED BUTTER

1/2 TSP. CINNAMON OR NUTMEG

2 C APPLESAUCE

DASH SALT

3 EGGS, SEPARATE

1 - 15 OZ. CAN SWEETENED
    CONDENSED MILK

2 TBLSP. LEMON JUICE

GRATES 1 LEMON

MIX CRUMBS, BUTTER AND CINNAMON; SPREAD HALF IN A
GREASED 8" SQUARE PAN. BEAT EGG YOLKS WELL; ADD
MILK, LEMON JUICE, RIND, SALT AND APPLESAUCE; FOLD IN
STIFFLY BEATEN EGG WHITES. POUR MIX IN PAN AND TOP
WITH REST OF CRUMBS. BAKE AT 350° FOR 50 MINUTES. SERVE
WARM OR COLD TOPPED WITH WHIPPED CREAM.

CRUNCH PUFF PUDDING

1/4 C BUTTER

1/2 C SUGAR

2 EGGS, SEPARATE

1 TSP. GRATED LEMON RIND

3 TBLSP. LEMON JUICE

2 TBLSP. FLOUR

1/4 C NON FAT DRY MILK

1/4 C GRAPENUTS   1 C FLUID MILK

CREAM BUTTER WITH SUGAR. ADD EGG YOLKS AND BEAT WELL.
ADD LEMON RIND AND JUICE. STIR IN FLOUR, DRY MILK, GRAPE-
NUTS AND FLUID MILK. BEAT WHITES UNTIL STIFF AND FOLD INTO
GRAPENUTS MIX. TURN INTO A GREASED 1 1/2 QT. CASSEROLE.
PLACE IN PAN OF HOT WATER. BAKE AT 325° FOR ONE HOUR AND
15 MINUTES. SERVE WARM OR COLD, WITH WHIPPED CREAM.

LEMON SOUFFLE

1 C SUGAR   2 TBLSP. MELTED BUTTER   GRATES 1 LEMON

4 TBLSP. FLOUR   3 STIFFLY BEATEN EGG WHITES   1/2 C MILK

1/8 TSP. SALT   5 TBLSP. LEMON JUICE   3 BEATEN YOLKS

BLEND SUGAR, FLOUR, SALT, BUTTER, LEMON JUICE, RIND,
YOLKS AND MILK. FOLD IN WHITES. POUR INTO A WELL-GREASED
BAKING DISH. PLACE IN A PAN OF HOT WATER. BAKE AT
350° FOR 1 HOUR. SERVE WITH WHIPPED CREAM.

99

FRUIT CRISP

SLICE 1 QUART OF APPLES, PEACHES, PEARS (OR OTHER FRUIT) INTO A 9" PAN. SPRINKLE WITH CINNAMON SUGAR AND LEMON JUICE. BLEND TOGETHER: 1 C BROWN SUGAR, 1 C FLOUR, 1 TSP. BAKING PWD., 1 EGG

PAT THIS MIXTURE LIGHTLY ON THE FRUIT. MELT 1/3 C BUTTER AND POUR OVER ALL. BAKE AT 350° FOR 30 MINUTES UNTIL GOLDEN BROWN. SERVE WITH WHIPPED CREAM — WARM OR COOL. NUTS MAY BE ADDED TO THE FLOUR MIX IF YOU WISH.

EASY COBBLER

PLACE ONE QUART OF FRUIT IN A CASSEROLE AND SPRINKLE WITH 2 TBLSP. FLOUR (3 TBLSP IF USING BERRIES), 1½ TSP. SALT, ½ C CORN SYRUP, HONEY OR TABLE SYRUP AND 2 TSP. LEMON JUICE. MIX: 1½ C BISQUICK, 3 TBLSP. SUGAR AND 2 TBLSP. BUTTER (CUT IN). STIR IN ½ C MILK. TURN OUT ON FLOURED WAX PAPER AND ROLL TO THE SAME SHAPE AS THE CASSEROLE. TURN DOUGH ONTO THE FRUIT AND SPRINKLE WITH CINNAMON SUGAR. BAKE AT 400° FOR 20 MINUTES. SERVE WARM OR COLD WITH CREAM.

CHERRY SOG

1 GRAHAM CRACKER PIE CRUST   1/3 C LEMON JUICE
1 CAN SWEETENED CONDENSED MILK   1 TSP. VANILLA
1 - 8 OZ. PKG CREAM CHEESE   1 CAN CHERRY PIE FILLING

BEAT CREAM CHEESE AND MILK TOGETHER UNTIL SMOOTH. MIX IN LEMON JUICE AND VANILLA. POUR INTO GRAHAM CRUST THAT HAS BEEN SHAPED IN A 9" PIE PAN. CHILL AND COVER WITH CHERRIES BEFORE SERVING. BLUEBERRY PIE FILLING IS GOOD TOO.

RICE PUDDING

2 C COOKED RICE	1 TSP. VANILLA
1 1/3 C MILK	4 EGGS
1/8 TSP. SALT	1/2 TSP. GRATED LEMON RIND
1/2 C BROWN SUGAR	1 TSP. LEMON JUICE
1 TBLSP. SOFT BUTTER	1/3 C RAISINS OR DATES

COMBINE AND BEAT MILK, SALT, BROWN SUGAR, BUTTER, VANILLA
AND EGGS. ADD TO RICE WITH LEMON JUICE AND RIND AND
RAISINS OR DATES. PLACE IN A BUTTERED CASSEROLE AND BAKE
AT 325° ABOUT 50 MINUTES. SERVE WITH A FRUIT SAUCE OR
WHIPPED CREAM.   OR

RICE CREAM

2 C COOKED RICE	1/3 C SUGAR
1 C MILK	1 TSP. VANILLA

MIX RICE, MILK, SUGAR AND VANILLA. FOLD IN TO THIS ENOUGH
WHIPPED CREAM TO MAKE THE RIGHT CONSISTENCY. SERVE WITH
A FRUIT SAUCE (CHERRY, FLAVORED WITH CHERRY HERRING) - 1/4 C
SLIVERED ALMONDS FOLDED IN OR AS A GARNISH. YOU MAY USE
INSTANT VANILLA PUDDING AND FOLD IN COOKED RICE AND WHIPPED
CREAM TO YOUR LIKING. AS A TOPPING YOU MIGHT LIKE TO USE
A 14 OZ. JAR OF LINGONBERRIES.

BAKED COFFEE SOUFFLE

2 TBLSP. BUTTER	2 TBLSP. INSTANT COFFEE	
2 TBLSP. FLOUR	3/4 C WATER	1/2 C SUGAR
1/4 TSP. SALT	3 EGGS, SEPARATE	1/2 TSP. VANILLA

MELT BUTTER. ADD FLOUR, SALT, COFFEE, AND WATER; STIR
AND COOK UNTIL THICK AND SMOOTH. REMOVE FROM HEAT. BEAT
YOLKS UNTIL LIGHT; ADD SUGAR GRADUALLY, BEATING WELL. STIR
IN COFFEE MIX AND VANILLA. BEAT EGG WHITES STIFF AND FOLD
INTO COFFEE MIXTURE. POUR INTO A GREASED 1 QT. CASSEROLE.
PLACE IN A PAN OF HOT WATER AND BAKE AT 350° - 50 MINUTES.
SERVE WITH CREAM.

101

INDIAN PUDDING (SERVES 8)

4 C MILK	1 TSP. CINNAMON	1/2 TSP. SALT
3/4 C YELLOW CORNMEAL	1/2 TSP. NUTMEG	4 BEATEN EGGS
1/4 C MOLASSES	1 C LIGHT BROWN SUGAR	1 C SOUR CREAM
1 TSP. GINGER	1/2 C MELTED BUTTER	HEAVY CREAM

HEAT 3 C MILK IN TOP OF A DOUBLE BOILER. MIX THE OTHER 1 C
MILK WITH THE CORNMEAL. ADD TO HOT MILK AND STIR AND COOK
UNTIL SLIGHTLY THICK (5 MINUTES). REMOVE FROM HEAT. MIX
MOLASSES WITH SPICES AND STIR INTO CORNMEAL MIXTURE. ADD
BROWN SUGAR, BUTTER, SALT, EGGS AND SOUR CREAM. BLEND.
BAKE IN A 2 QUART BUTTERED DISH AT 275° FOR 2 HOURS OR
UNTIL A KNIFE INSERTED IN THE CENTER COMES OUT CLEAN. SERVE
WARM WITH CREAM.

CHOCOLATE SAUCE #1 (MAKES 1 C)

MELT 2 SQUARES OF BITTER CHOCOLATE IN SIX TBLSP. WATER
OVER LOW HEAT, STIRRING UNTIL SMOOTH. ADD 1/2 C SUGAR
AND A DASH OF SALT. COOK AND STIR UNTIL SMOOTH AND SLIGHTLY
THICK. STIR IN 3 TBLSP. BUTTER AND 1/2 TSP. VANILLA. COOL.

CHOCOLATE SAUCE #2

MELT 2 SQUARES BITTER CHOCOLATE IN 1 C LIGHT CORN SYRUP
OVER LOW HEAT. REMOVE FROM HEAT AND STIR IN 1/2 TSP. VANILLA
AND 1 TBLSP. BUTTER.

BUTTERSCOTCH SAUCE

BOIL TO THE CONSISTENCY OF HEAVY SYRUP: 1/3 C WHITE CORN
SYRUP, 3/4 C PACKED BROWN SUGAR, 2 TBLSP. BUTTER AND 1/8
TSP. SALT. COOL AND ADD 1/3 C EVAPORATED MILK OR LIGHT
CREAM. BEAT. SERVE WARM OR COLD.

YOGURT

3 c NONFAT PWD. MILK   1 TALL CAN EVAPORATED MILK
6 c BOILING WATER   3 TBLSP. PLAIN YOGURT

ADD BOILING WATER TO PWD. MILK AND BEAT WITH A WHISK.
ADD EVAPORATED MILK. COOL MIXTURE TO 110° TO 120°
(SAME TEMPERATURE AS A BABY'S BOTTLE). ADD 3 TBLSP.
PLAIN YOGURT AND MIX WELL. COVER AND WRAP IN A BLANKET
TO HOLD THE HEAT. LET SIT FIVE HOURS WITHOUT LOOKING.
REFRIGERATE.

PUDDING NOTES

CHEESECAKE

SEPARATE 3 EGGS AND BEAT THE YOLKS WITH 12 OZ. CREAM CHEESE AND 1 TSP. VANILLA. BEAT THE WHITES STIFF, GRADUALLY ADDING 3/4 C SUGAR. FOLD WHITES INTO THE CREAM CHEESE MIX. POUR INTO A 9" PIE PAN LINED WITH A GRAHAM CRACKER CRUST. BAKE AT 350° FOR 1/2 HOUR. TURN OFF HEAT AND ALLOW TO COOL IN OVEN. <u>TOPPING</u>: MIX 1/2 PINT SOUR CREAM WITH 2 TBLSP. SUGAR AND 1/4 TSP. VANILLA. SPREAD ON CHEESECAKE AND BAKE AGAIN AT 350° FOR TEN MINUTES.

<u>HELEN'S PUMPKIN CHEESECAKE</u>   (OVEN 325°)

1/4 C GRAHAM CRACKER CRUMBS	1 CAN (1 LB.) PUMPKIN
4 PKG. (8 OZ.) SOFTENED CREAM CHEESE	1 TSP. CINNAMON
1 1/2 C SUGAR	1/2 TSP. NUTMEG
5 LARGE EGGS 1/4 TSP. SALT	1/4 TSP. CLOVES
1/4 C FLOUR	1/4 TSP. GINGER

BUTTER A 9" SPRING FORM PAN GENEROUSLY. SPRINKLE WITH GRAHAM CRUMBS — SHAKE TO COAT ALL SIDES. BEAT CHEESE UNTIL FLUFFY. GRADUALLY BEAT IN SUGAR. ADD EGGS, ONE AT A TIME, MIXING WELL AFTER EACH. BEAT IN FLOUR, SALT AND SPICES. POUR INTO PREPARED PAN. BAKE 1 1/2 HOUR OR UNTIL FIRM AROUND SIDES, BUT SOFT IN THE CENTER. TURN OFF HEAT. OPEN OVEN DOOR AND LET CAKE COOL IN OVEN THIRTY MINUTES. REMOVE FROM OVEN AND COOL COMPLETELY ON RACK. CHILL. THE FLAVOR IS BETTER THE SECOND DAY.

PIES AND CRUSTS

NEVER FAIL PIE CRUST (2 - 9" CRUSTS)

SIFT 2 C FLOUR AND 1 TSP SALT. REMOVE 1/3 C AND MIX WITH 1/4 C WATER TO FORM A PASTE. CUT 2/3 C CRISCO INTO THE REMAINING FLOUR UNTIL IT'S LIKE COARSE MEAL. ADD THE PASTE AND MIX UNTIL IT ALL CLINGS TOGETHER. DIVIDE IN HALF AND FORM INTO BALLS. ROLL OUT ON A FLOURED BOARD.

ADVENTURE CRUST (2 - 9" CRUSTS)

2 1/2 C FLOUR   1 TSP. SALT   1/2 C MILK
1/2 C LARD   1 1/2 TBLSP. VINEGAR

SOUR THE MILK WITH VINEGAR. MIX FLOUR AND SALT AND CUT THE LARD IN. ADD MILK TO FLOUR MIX ALL AT ONCE. FORM INTO A DOUGH, HANDLING GENTLY. ROLL OUT.

THERE'S AN INFINITE VARIETY OF CRUMB CRUSTS TO BE MADE USING DIFFERENT TYPES OF COOKIES OR CEREALS. THE GRAHAM CRACKER CRUST IS THE MOST WIDELY USED. NOW, WHY NOT TRY ONE OF THE FOLLOWING FOR A CHANGE.

KIND	BUTTER	CRUMBS	SUGAR
16-18 GRAHAM CRACKERS	1/4 LB.	1 1/3 C	1/4 C
16 CHOCOLATE OREOS	1/4 C	1 1/3 C	0
19 CHOCOLATE WAFERS	1/4 C	1 1/3 C	0
24 VANILLA WAFERS	1/4 C	1 1/3 C	0
18 SHORTBREAD COOKIES	2 TBLSP.	1 1/4 C	0
14 OATMEAL COOKIES	1/4 C	1 1/4 C	0
20 GINGERSNAPS	1/3 C	1 1/3 C	0
14 CHOCOLATE CHIP COOKIES	2 TBLSP.	1 1/4 C	0
CEREAL FLAKES	1/4 C	1 1/3 C	2 TBLSP.
ROLLED OATS	1/3 C	1 1/4 C	1/3 C BROWN

105

CRUSH COOKIES OR CEREAL BETWEEN WAXED PAPER. MIX IN SUGAR AND WORK IN SOFT BUTTER WITH A FORK. PRESS INTO A PIE TIN (YOU MAY SET ASIDE A COUPLE OF TBLSP. FOR TOPPING, DEPENDING ON THE FILLING). WITH ANY OF THEM, YOU CAN REDUCE THE CRUMBS TO 1 C AND ADD ½ C FINELY CHOPPED WALNUTS, PECANS, ALMONDS OR BRAZIL NUTS. WITH OATMEAL, ADD A COUPLE TBLSP. OF WHEAT GERM. OTHER ADDITIONS THAT ARE INTERESTING TO A CRUST: 1 TBLSP POPPY OR SESAME SEED, 1 TSP. GRATED CITRUS RIND OR REDUCE CRUMBS ¼ C AND ADD COCONUT.

APPLE PIE

LINE PIE PAN WITH PASTRY. MIX TOGETHER ⅔ C WHITE OR BROWN SUGAR, ⅛ TSP. SALT, 2 TBLSP. FLOUR (OR 1½ TBLSP. CORNSTARCH). TOSS GENTLY WITH SIX C SLICED TART APPLES. PLACE IN LAYERS IN SHELL. DOT WITH 1½ TBLSP. BUTTER AND SPRINKLE WITH 1 TBLSP. LEMON JUICE. COVER WITH TOP CRUST OR STREUSEL TOPPING: ½ C LIGHT BROWN SUGAR, ¼ C BUTTER, ⅓ C FLOUR AND ¼ TSP. CINNAMON. MIX WITH FINGERS TO CONSISTENCY OF COARSE CRUMBS. PAT ON TOP OF APPLES. BAKE AT 450° FOR TEN MINUTES, THEN AT 350° FOR ABOUT 40 MINUTES. IF USING REGULAR CRUST, BRUSH WITH MILK BEFORE BAKING.

BLUEBERRY PIE

LINE PIE PAN WITH PASTRY. COMBINE 3 TBLSP. QUICK-COOKING TAPIOCA WITH ⅔ C SUGAR. BLEND GENTLY WITH ONE QUART OF BLUEBERRIES. LET STAND FIFTEEN MINUTES, THEN SEASON WITH 1½ TBLSP. LEMON JUICE AND ½ TSP. CINNAMON (OPTIONAL). FILL PIE SHELL WITH BERRIES, DOT WITH BUTTER AND COVER WITH THE TOP CRUST. BAKE AT 450° FOR TEN MINUTES AND THEN AT 350° FOR 40 MINUTES.

Sometimes we'll use combinations of fruits in a pie. Blueberry-peach is a favorite. Peach pie is nice if flavored with almond. Peach pie takes less sugar than apple. Rhubarb pie needs more. — To 4 c rhubarb, use 1/4 c flour and 1 1/2 - 2 c sugar, 1 tblsp. butter, and grated orange rind.

PUMPKIN PIE

1 1/4 c pumpkin	1/2 tsp. nutmeg	3/4 c evaporated milk
1 c brown sugar	1/2 tsp. salt	1/4 c molasses
1 tblsp. flour	3 beaten eggs	9" unbaked pie shell
1 tsp. ginger	grates of 1 orange	8 walnut halves
1/2 tsp. cinnamon	1/2 c orange juice	

Combine pumpkin, sugar, flour, spices, salt, eggs, rind, juice, molasses and milk. Pour into shell. Float walnuts on top. Bake at 450° for 15 minutes. Reduce heat to 350° and bake 30 minutes more, or until firm.

COTTAGE CHEESE PIE

2 c cottage cheese	Juice of 2 oranges
Rind 1 lemon	3 eggs, beaten
Juice 1 lemon	1/4 tsp. salt 1 c sugar

Seive cottage cheese and add everything else. Mix and pour into a pastry-lined 9" pie pan. Bake at 450° for 10 minutes, then at 350° for 25 minutes until firm.

PECAN PIE

Beat 3 eggs very light. Slowly beat in 3/4 c sugar, 1/4 c melted butter, 1 c brown corn syrup, 1/2 tsp. salt and 1 tsp. vanilla. Stir in 1 c broken pecans and pour into a pie shell that has been pre-baked at 450° for five minutes. Bake at 375° for 40 minutes until firm.

107

QUICK CUSTARD PIE

2 C MILK   4 EGGS   1 1/2 TSP. VANILLA

1/2 C SUGAR   1/4 C BUTTER   1/2 C BISQUICK

BEAT ALL TOGETHER AND POUR INTO A GREASED, FLOURED
9" PIE PAN. BAKE AT 375° UNTIL SET ~ 30-40 MINUTES.
SPRINKLE NUTMEG ON TOP. CUSTARD WILL RISE AND A CRUST
FORM ON THE BOTTOM. TO VARY, ADD COCONUT OR NUTS.

LEMON CURD PIE

4 LARGE EGGS   1/4 C SOFT BUTTER

1/8 TSP. SALT   2 TBLSP. GRATED LEMON PEEL

1 3/4 C SUGAR   1/2 C LEMON JUICE

BEAT EGGS IN THE TOP OF A DOUBLE BOILER. STIR IN SALT, SUGAR,
BUTTER, LEMON PEEL AND JUICE. COOK OVER HOT WATER ABOUT
30 MINUTES, STIRRING FREQUENTLY, UNTIL THICK AND SMOOTH.
WHEN COOL, FOLD IN 1 C WHIPPED CREAM OR COOL WHIP AND
PILE IN COOKED PIE CRUST. OR PUT IN SHELL AS IS AND TOP
WITH SOUR CREAM OR WHIPPED CREAM.

BANANA - SPLIT PIE

1 BAKED PIE SHELL (CHOCOLATE, GRAHAM OR REGULAR).
BEAT 2 EGGS WITH 2 C PWD. SUGAR. LET SIT 15 MINUTES.
POUR INTO PIE SHELL. ADD A LAYER OF 2 SLICED BANANAS.
DRAIN WELL 1 CAN CRUSHED PINEAPPLE AND SPREAD IT ON TOP OF
BANANAS. TOP WITH WHIPPED CREAM OR DREAM WHIP. SPRINKLE
WITH CHOPPED PECANS AND CHOCOLATE SPRINKLES. SCATTER A
FEW CHERRIES ON TOP.

Adventure Ice Cream

1½ C SUGAR   3 C HEAVY CREAM

5 EGGS, BEATEN   2 C WHOLE MILK

2 TSP. VANILLA   1 C EVAPORATED MILK

MIX ALL TOGETHER AND FILL FREEZER CAN 2/3 FULL.
THIS MAKES ENOUGH FOR TEN PEOPLE.

NOTES

COOKING FOR A WINDJAMMER MOB LIMITS FIXING EGGS MANY DIFFERENT WAYS. THE SIMPLEST METHOD IS TO SCRAMBLE. THERE ARE ENDLESS VARIATIONS.

2 EGGS PER PERSON ARE STIRRED UP (WITH 1 TBLSP. WATER OR MILK PER EGG). SEASONINGS ARE ADDED — SALT, PEPPER, HERBS OR SEEDS.

① CHOPPED ONIONS AND GREEN PEPPERS SAUTÉED IN BUTTER. ADD EGGS AND COOK AND STIR UNTIL SET.

② TO THE ABOVE, STIR IN CHOPPED TOMATO AND SPRINKLE THE TOP WITH GRATED CHEDDAR CHEESE AND/OR CHOPPED PARSLEY.

③ COTTAGE CHEESE AND CHIVES MAY BE STIRRED INTO THE EGGS WHILE COOKING.

④ CREAM OF MUSHROOM SOUP OR CREAM OF CELERY SOUP MAY BE ADDED WHILE COOKING. DECORATE WITH CHOPPED PIMIENTO, SPRINKLE WITH PAPRIKA.

⑤ HEAVY CREAM OR CHUNKS OF CREAM CHEESE MAKE THE EGGS SO SMOOTH AND SOUR CREAM GIVES A LOVELY TASTE.

⑥ IF YOU SPROUT MUNG BEANS OR ALFALFA SEEDS, TRY STIR-FRYING THEM A COUPLE OF MINUTES WITH A LITTLE GRATED ONION BEFORE ADDING THE EGGS.

⑦ SESAME, POPPY, CARAWAY OR DILL SEED ADD AN INTERESTING FLAVOR TO SCRAMBLED EGGS.

⑧ DON'T FORGET MUSHROOMS — THEY'RE GOOD ANY WAY! EGGS ARE SUCH A MARVELOUS CARRIER AND YOUR BREAKFAST MAY HAVE A "HUEVOS RANCHEROS" TOUCH OR COME OUT WITH A CHINESE TASTE. THE ONLY LIMIT IS YOUR IMAGINATION.

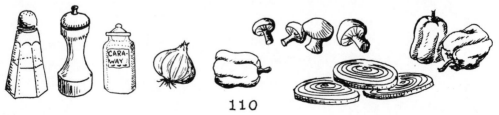

MUSHROOM-EGG POACH (SERVES 6)

SAUTÉ 1 MEDIUM CHOPPED ONION IN 2 TBLSP.
BUTTER IN A SKILLET. ADD 1 CAN CREAM
OF MUSHROOM SOUP, 1 CAN CHEDDAR CHEESE
SOUP, 1 SMALL CAN MUSHROOM PIECES, AND
3/4 SOUP CAN MILK. HEAT ALL TO A BOIL,

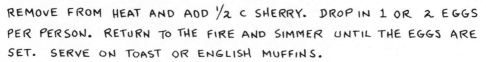

REMOVE FROM HEAT AND ADD 1/2 C SHERRY. DROP IN 1 OR 2 EGGS
PER PERSON. RETURN TO THE FIRE AND SIMMER UNTIL THE EGGS ARE
SET. SERVE ON TOAST OR ENGLISH MUFFINS.

RED-EYE POACH (SERVES 6)

SAUTÉ 1 MEDIUM CHOPPED ONION, 1/2 CHOPPED GREEN PEPPER AND
1 MINCED CLOVE GARLIC IN 2 TBLSP. BUTTER IN A SKILLET. ADD 2
CANS (1 LB.) STEWED TOMATOES, 1 TBLSP. WORCESTERSHIRE SAUCE
AND 1/2 TSP. BASIL. BRING TO A BOIL, LOWER THE HEAT AND DROP
IN 1 OR 2 EGGS PER PERSON. SPRINKLE ON TOP 1/2 C GRATED
AMERICAN CHEESE. SIMMER UNTIL EGGS ARE SET. SERVE ON TOAST.
A MEXICAN VARIATION IS TO ADD 1 ENVELOPE OF TACO SEASONING MIX
TO THE TOMATOES AND SIMMER THIS MIXTURE FOR FIVE MINUTES
BEFORE DROPPING IN THE EGGS. — MUY SABROSA!

CREAMED EGGS (SERVES 6)

3 TBLSP. BUTTER	1 TBLSP. WORCESTERSHIRE
1 MEDIUM ONION, CHOPPED	1/2 C GRATED AMERICAN CHEESE
1/2 GREEN PEPPER, CHOPPED	SALT AND PEPPER TO TASTE
1/4 C FLOUR	1 CAN CREAM OF MUSHROOM SOUP
1 1/2 C MILK	PARSLEY

_ _ _ _ _ 6 COARSE-CHOPPED HARD BOILED EGGS _ _ _ _ _ _

SAUTÉ ONION AND GREEN PEPPER IN BUTTER IN A SAUCEPAN. REMOVE
FROM FIRE AND STIR IN FLOUR. GRADUALLY STIR IN MILK. RETURN TO
FIRE AND STIR AND COOK UNTIL THICK AND SMOOTH. STIR IN WORCESTER-
SHIRE, CHEESE, SALT, PEPPER AND MUSHROOM SOUP. IF TOO THICK, THIN
WITH MILK. ADD EGGS AND PARSLEY. SERVE ON HOT, SPLIT BISCUITS
— OR ON TOAST.

On "ADVENTURE", WE SOMETIMES FIXED A "BUCKEYE BRUNCH" (A NAME STOLEN FROM SCHOONER "HARVEY GAMAGE"). IT'S AN OVEN FONDUE, WHICH IS BAKED FOR BREAKFAST, BUT MAY BE LAID UP THE NIGHT BEFORE.

BUCKEYE BRUNCH (SERVES 6-8)

BUTTER A RECTANGULAR BAKING PAN. BUTTER TEN SLICES OF BREAD (WE LIKE RYE) AND CUT IN CUBES. BEAT 6 EGGS WELL AND ADD 3 C MILK, 2 TBLSP. PARSLEY, 1 TSP. DRY MUSTARD, 1 TSP. SALT. MIX BREAD AND EGG MIXTURE AND ADD 2 C SHREDDED AMERICAN CHEESE. SPREAD IN PAN AND BAKE AT 350° FOR AN HOUR OR UNTIL SET.

VARIATIONS: MIX IN 1-2 C COOKED CHOPPED HAM. FOR LUNCH, YOU MAY ADD 3 TBLSP. FINE CHOPPED ONION AND 1 PKG. CHOPPED FROZEN SPINACH. — GRATED RAW ZUCHINNI IS A WINNER TOO.

SAUSAGE BUCK (SERVES 6)

8 EGGS, SLIGHTLY BEATEN

6 SLICES BREAD, CUBED

1 LB. SAUSAGE, COOKED AND CRUMBLED

2 C MILK

1 C CHEDDAR CHEESE, GRATED

1 TSP. SALT

1 TSP. DRY MUSTARD

½ GREEN PEPPER, DICED

1 SMALL ONION, DICED

MIX ALL INGREDIENTS TOGETHER AND PUT IN A GREASED 9 X 13" PAN. REFRIGERATE OVERNIGHT. BAKE AT 350° FOR 35 MINUTES OR UNTIL FIRM.

QUICHE

1 - 9" PIE SHELL. PRICK WITH A FORK, BRUSH WITH EGG WHITE (BEATEN TO A FROTH) AND BAKE AT 400° ABOUT SEVEN MINUTES. FOR FILLING: SAUTÉ ½ LB. BACON (CUT IN 1" PIECES) UNTIL ALMOST CRISP. DRAIN. SCALD 2 C MILK OR CREAM. COOL A LITTLE AND BEAT WITH 3 EGGS, ¼ TSP. SALT, DASH PEPPER, DASH CAYENNE, A GRATING OF NUTMEG AND LASTLY, ADD 1 TBLSP. CHOPPED CHIVES. SPRINKLE BACON AND 1 C DICED SWISS CHEESE IN PIE SHELL. POUR CUSTARD OVER. BAKE AT 375° FOR 35-40 MINUTES.

QUICHE WAS USED AS A LUNCHEON DISH AND WITH VARIATIONS:

HAM — SUBSTITUTE CHOPPED HAM FOR THE BACON AND ADD ½ TSP. DRY MUSTARD TO THE LIQUID.

VEGETABLE — SAUTÉ IN 1 TBLSP. BUTTER ¾ C SLICED ONION AND SPREAD ON CHEESE WITH ½ SLICED GREEN PEPPER.

OTHER VEGETABLES — SPREAD ON CHEESE 1 C CHOPPED SPINACH, OR GRATED ZUCCHINI, OR MUSHROOMS, OR DRAINED CUT TOMATOES.

SEAFOOD — SPREAD ON CHEESE 1 C CHOPPED LOBSTER, SHRIMP, CLAMS, CHUNKS OF TUNA OR SALMON IN PLACE OF THE BACON.

EGG NOTES

SALADS

TANGY SLAW (SERVES 4)

3 C SHREDDED CABBAGE	½ C SOUR CREAM	1 ½ TBLSP. SUGAR
2 TBLSP. GRATED ONION	1 ½ TSP. SALT	¼ TSP. PAPRIKA
1 TSP. CELERY SEED	DASH CAYENNE	4 TBLSP. VINEGAR
½ C MAYONNAISE	1 TSP. DRY MUSTARD	1 TSP. CARAWAY SEED

MIX ALL TOGETHER AND LET SIT AN HOUR OR SO BEFORE SERVING.
DILL SEED MAY BE USED IN PLACE OF CARAWAY IF YOU WISH. GRATED
CARROTS MAY BE ADDED FOR COLOR.

PINEAPPLE SLAW (SERVES 4)

3 C SHREDDED CABBAGE	¼ C CHOPPED MARASCHINO CHERRIES
1 C MINIATURE MARSHMALLOWS	½ C MAYONNAISE
1 - 11 OZ. CAN DRAINED CRUSHED PINEAPPLE	½ C WHIPPED CREAM

MIX ALL TOGETHER AND SERVE.

ANDREA'S WILTED SPINACH (SERVES 4)

1 LB. SPINACH	2 TBLSP. SUGAR
4 SLICES BACON, DICED	½ TSP. SALT
⅓ C VINEGAR	DASH PEPPER
1 HARD BOILED EGG, CHOPPED	⅓ C WATER

CLEAN SPINACH AND BREAK INTO LARGE PIECES IN A
BOWL. FRY BACON, DRAIN AND RESERVE. MIX AND
HEAT VINEGAR, WATER, SUGAR, SALT AND PEPPER.
MIX EGG AND BACON INTO SPINACH. POUR HOT
VINEGAR MIXTURE OVER JUST BEFORE SERVING.

RICE SALAD   (SERVES 4)

2 C COOKED RICE

1/4 C SALAD OIL

1/4 C WINE VINEGAR

6 WATER CHESTNUTS, CHOPPED

1/2 C MINCED PARSLEY

1/4 C MINCED GREEN ONION

1/2 GREEN PEPPER, CHOPPED

1/2 C CHOPPED CELERY

1 TSP. MIXED HERBS

SALT AND PEPPER

STIR OIL AND VINEGAR INTO RICE WHILE HOT. COOL AND ADD THE
REST OF THE INGREDIENTS. SEASON TO TASTE AND DRESS
WITH 1/2 C GREEN GODDESS DRESSING.

RICE AND BEAN SALAD   (SERVES 6)

1/2 C SALAD OIL

1/2 C WINE VINEGAR

2 TBLSP. SUGAR

1 TSP. SALT

1 C DICED CELERY

1/2 GREEN PEPPER, CHOPPED

1/2 TSP. PEPPER

1 CAN RED KIDNEY BEANS, DRAINED

1 CAN CUT GREEN BEANS, DRAINED

1 MEDIUM RED ONION, THINLY SLICED

3 PIMIENTOS, DICED

2 C COOKED COLD RICE

BLEND OIL, VINEGAR, SUGAR, SALT AND PEPPER. IN A BOWL, MIX
CELERY, GREEN PEPPER, KIDNEY BEANS, GREEN BEANS, ONION,
PIMIENTO AND RICE. POUR OIL-VINEGAR MIXTURE OVER VEGETABLES
AND REFRIGERATE A COUPLE OF HOURS BEFORE SERVING.

POTATO SALAD IDEAS

BOIL UP POTATOES ENOUGH FOR YOUR GROUP. DRAIN, AND WHILE
POTATOES ARE HOT, POUR OVER FRENCH OR ITALIAN DRESSING
AND MIX GENTLY. COOL. THEN ADD MINCED ONION, CHOPPED
CELERY AND GREEN PEPPER. SEASON WITH SALT, PEPPER,
SEASON ALL, FINES HERBS, PARSLEY, MUSTARD AND MAYONNAISE.
DILL SEED IS AN INTERESTING ADDITION. GARNISH WITH
CHOPPED HARD BOILED EGGS AND CRUMBLED BACON.

ROAST BEEF SALAD

(COURTESY OF THE "HARVEY GAMAGE") — A GREAT USE
FOR LEFT-OVER ROAST BEEF.   PROPORTIONS ARE A LITTLE
LOOSE, DEPENDING ON THE AMOUNT OF BEEF YOU HAVE. MIX CHUNKS
OF COOKED ROAST BEEF WITH CHOPPED TOMATOES, CHOPPED ONION
AND PARSLEY. MAKE A DRESSING OF $2/3$ C SALAD OIL, 3 TBLSP.
RED WINE VINEGAR AND $1\frac{1}{2}$ TBLSP. DIJON MUSTARD. SHAKE
UP AND TOSS WITH SALAD. SALT AND PEPPER TO TASTE. DEPENDING
ON QUANTITIES INVOLVED, YOU MIGHT NEED MORE (OR LESS)
DRESSING.

GREEN SALADS

THE USUAL ASSORTMENT OF GREENS ARE BROKEN UP AND ADDITIONS
DEPEND ON WHAT IS ON HAND AND MOOD — CUCUMBERS, TOMATO
WEDGES, RADISHES, GREEN PEPPER, CARROTS. IF WE'VE SPROUTED
MUNG BEANS OR ALFALFA SEEDS, THEY'RE ADDED. TRY ADDING A
HANDFUL OF SUNFLOWER SEEDS. RAW SLICED MUSHROOMS ARE
SUPER.   SEASONED CROUTONS ARE KEPT ON THE SHELF AND TOSSED
ON AT THE LAST MINUTE.   WE SOMETIMES USE GOOD SEASONS
DRESSING MIXES, OR MAKE OUR OWN.   HERE ARE TWO TO TRY:

TOMATO FRENCH DRESSING

1 CAN TOMATO SOUP	½ C VINEGAR	1 TBLSP. DRY MUSTARD
1 CAN SALAD OIL	⅛ TSP. GARLIC PWD.	SALT AND PEPPER
1 C SUGAR	2 TBLSP. CELERY SEED	

BEAT ALL TOGETHER WELL WITH A WHISK OR SHAKE IN A JAR.

GARLIC DRESSING

1 CLOVE GARLIC, PRESSED	1 TSP. SALT
1 TBLSP. OLIVE OIL	1 TSP. ACCENT
2 TBLSP. LEMON JUICE	6 SHAKES TABASCO

MIX ALL TOGETHER AND SHAKE WELL.

116

FRUIT SALADS

SUMMERTIME IN NEW ENGLAND GIVES AN ABUNDANCE OF FRESH FRUITS.
COMBINATIONS DEPEND ON WHAT'S "IN", BUT THERE ARE MELONS, PLUMS,
PEARS, GRAPES, CITRUS, CHERRIES, APPLES AND BERRIES. MOST WEEKS
FRUIT IS HEAPED IN A SCALLOPED WATERMELON RIND TO SERVE WITH
A **DRESSING** OF :

1 C SOUR CREAM	1 TBLSP. LEMON JUICE
1 C WHIPPED CREAM	1 TBLSP. PWD. SUGAR
½ TSP. CINNAMON	

ORANGE - ONION SALAD

DON'T KNOCK IT UNTIL YOU TRY IT ! - ORANGE SECTIONS ON A BED
OF LETTUCE WITH RED ONION RINGS. SERVE WITH FRENCH DRESSING.

LIME - CHEESE MOLD

1 PKG. LIME JELLO	2 C CRUSHED PINEAPPLE	2 TSP. HORSERADISH
1 PKG. LEMON JELLO	1 C MILK	1 C COTTAGE CHEESE
2 C HOT WATER	1 C CHOPPED NUTS	1 C MAYONNAISE

DISSOLVE JELLO IN HOT WATER AND LET COOL. ADD DRAINED PINEAPPLE.
COMBINE MILK, NUTS, CHEESE AND MAYONNAISE. WHEN JELLO IS
PARTIALLY SET, MIX THE TWO TOGETHER. ADD HORSERADISH. PLACE IN
A MOLD AND CHILL UNTIL FIRM.

NOTES

117

SANDWICHES & STUFFINGS

CHICKEN OR TURKEY

2 C DICED CHICKEN OR TURKEY	1/4 C TOASTED SLIVERED ALMONDS
1 C SLICED CELERY	2 CHOPPED GREEN ONIONS
1/4 C FRENCH DRESSING	1/2 C MAYONNAISE
SALT AND PEPPER	1/4 C SOUR CREAM

MARINATE MEAT AND CELERY IN FRENCH DRESSING AN HOUR OR SO. SEASON WITH SALT AND PEPPER, GREEN ONIONS AND ALMONDS. DRESS WITH MAYONNAISE MIXED WITH SOUR CREAM. VARY WITH CURRY PWD. OR ADD 1 C COOKED RICE. IT'S DELICIOUS IF YOU ADD 1 C HALVED SEEDED GRAPES.

EGG SALAD

6 HARD BOILED EGGS	1 TSP. CARAWAY OR DILL SEED
1/2 C CHOPPED CELERY	1/4 TSP. SEASON ALL
1 TSP. MUSTARD	1/4 TSP. GARLIC PWD.
2 TBLSP. CHOPPED CHIVES	MAYONNAISE
SALT AND PEPPER TO TASTE	SOUR CREAM

CHOP EGGS FINE AND ADD THE REMAINING INGREDIENTS, USING HALF MAYONNAISE AND HALF SOUR CREAM TO GIVE THE PROPER CONSISTENCY. YOU MAY VARY THIS BY ADDING 1 TSP. CURRY PWD. AND/OR 1/4 C RELISH.

HAM SALAD

GRIND WITH THE FINE BLADE OF A MEAT GRINDER — LEFTOVER HAM AND/OR LUNCHEON MEAT. MIX IN CHOPPED CELERY, MINCED ONION, CHOPPED GREEN PEPPER, WORCESTERSHIRE, MUSTARD AND MAYONNAISE. MEASUREMENTS DEPEND ON YOUR OWN LIKES. OTHER ADDITIONS ARE CHOPPED PICKLES OR CHOPPED PINEAPPLE AND WALNUTS. IF YOU ADD PINEAPPLE, GRATE IN A LITTLE NUTMEG TOO.

TUNA SALAD

2 CANS CHUNK TUNA (7 OZ.)	½ C MAYONNAISE
⅓ C SWEET CHOPPED PICKLE	½ C SOUR CREAM
2 TBLSP. MINCED GREEN PEPPER	½ TSP. SALT ✦ DASH PEPPER
1 C FINE CHOPPED CELERY	2 TBLSP. LEMON JUICE
2 TBLSP. PARSLEY	DASH CAYENNE

MIX ALL TOGETHER. I LIKE TO ADD ½ C CHOPPED APPLE TOO.

SEASONED TOAST

(GREAT TO SERVE WITH SOUP OR AS A CHANGE FROM GARLIC BREAD)
FOR 15 PIECES OF TOAST — MIX:

¾ C SOFTENED BUTTER OR OLEO	¼ TSP. FINES HERBS
1 CHOPPED MEDIUM ONION	¼ TSP. SEASON ALL
1 TBLSP. CHOPPED PARSLEY	1 TSP. WORCESTERSHIRE
2 TSP. SESAME SEED	DASH PEPPER
2 TSP. POPPY SEED	¼ C PARMESAN CHEESE

SPREAD ON BREAD, OVERLAP THE SLICES SLIGHTLY ON BAKING
SHEETS AND BAKE AT 400° UNTIL TOASTED.

Stuffings

STUFFINGS ARE ANOTHER REMINDER OF GRANDMA'S KITCHEN AND
FESTIVE HOLIDAY TIMES. IN FACT, MANY PEOPLE
NEVER HAVE STUFFING UNLESS IT'S THANKSGIVING
OR CHRISTMAS AND THERE'S A TURKEY IN THE OFFING.
THERE ARE MANY DIFFERENT WAYS TO FIX A
STUFFING AND IT'S A MARVELOUS SIDE DISH WITH
ALMOST ANY MEAT OR FISH. IT MAY BE VARIED
DEPENDING ON WHAT'S AROUND IN THE LEFTOVER
DEPARTMENT.

CORN BREAD STUFFING (10 CUPS)

1 LB. BULK SAUSAGE	1 CHOPPED GREEN PEPPER	1 TSP. SALT
6 C CORNBREAD	1 1/4 C CHICKEN STOCK	1/2 TSP. PEPPER
6 C BREADCRUMBS	1/2 TSP. SAGE	2 LG. ONIONS, CHOP
2 C SLICED CELERY	1/2 TSP. THYME	3 PARSLEY SPRIGS

FRY SAUSAGE AND DRAIN. IN SAUSAGE FAT, SAUTÉ ONIONS UNTIL
SOFT. TOAST BREADS AND COMBINE WITH ALL THE INGREDIENTS. IF
YOU LIKE, ADD 1/3 C CHOPPED RED PIMIENTO. THIS IS GOOD WITH
POULTRY, PORK OR HAM.

TRADITIONAL STUFFING

2 QTS. DRY BREAD, BROKEN UP (ANY KIND OF BREAD WILL DO)

1/2 C WHEAT GERM	1/2 C CHOPPED ONION	1/2 TSP. THYME
1/2 C DICED CELERY	1 TSP. SALT	1/2 TSP. POULTRY SEASONING
2 TBLSP PARSLEY	1/2 TSP. PEPPER	3/4 TO 1 C CHICKEN BROTH
1 LB. BULK SAUSAGE	1/2 TSP. EACH SAGE AND MARJORAM	

FRY SAUSAGE AND DRAIN. IN SAUSAGE FAT, SAUTÉ ONIONS UNTIL SOFT.
ADD ONION TO BREAD WITH THE REMAINING INGREDIENTS. YOU MAY
ADD 1/2 C CHOPPED NUTS AND/OR 1/2 C RAISINS OR CURRANTS.

RICE STUFFING (5C)

6 SLICES BACON, CHOPPED	1 C CHOPPED CELERY	1/2 C MILK
1/4 C CHOPPED ONION	3/4 TSP. SALT	1/2 C CREAM
4 C COOKED RICE	1/4 TSP. PEPPER	(OR 1 C CHICKEN STOCK)
1 C DRY BREAD CRUMBS	1/8 TSP. SAGE	2 TBLSP. PARSLEY

SAUTÉ BACON WITH ONIONS. POUR OFF ALL BUT 2 TBLSP. GREASE.
MIX WITH REMAINING INGREDIENTS. IF YOU LIKE, ADD 1/2 C PINE
NUTS.

STUFFING FOR FISH (4C)

MIX - 5 C DRY BREAD CRUMBS, 1/4 C CHOPPED CHIVES, 1 C
CHOPPED CELERY (WITH LEAVES), 1/4 C CHOPPED PARSLEY,
1/2 C CHOPPED WATERCRESS AND 3 BEATEN EGGS.

SEASON WITH - SALT, PAPRIKA, 3/4 TSP. TARRAGON OR DILL
SEED, 3 TBLSP. CAPERS AND 1/4 TSP. NUTMEG.

ADD - ENOUGH MILK, MELTED BUTTER OR SOUP STOCK TO MAKE
A LOOSE STUFFING.

YOU MAY ADD MORE VEGETABLES TO THIS DRESSING - CHOPPED
TOMATOES OR MUSHROOMS, OR GRATED CARROT.

FRUIT STUFFING

SAUTÉ 5 MEDIUM CHOPPED ONIONS AND 5 CHOPPED APPLES WITH
5 SLICES CHOPPED BACON. ADD 1 MINCED CLOVE GARLIC. YOU
MAY ADD 1 CAN DICED PEACHES, A SMALL CAN DICED PINEAPPLE
AND A FEW CHERRIES. - MANDARIN ORANGES ARE NICE.
SPRINKLE WITH THYME, SALT, PEPPER, SAGE AND PARSLEY.
ADD RAISINS AND WALNUTS IF YOU WISH. BREAK UP 4 OR 5
SLICES OF BREAD AND MIX IN WITH 2 BEATEN EGGS...AND OH,
YES, A LITTLE SWEET BASIL.

PINEAPPLE STUFFING (GREAT WITH HAM)

1/4 LB. BUTTER	1/4 C SUGAR
6 SLICES CUBED BREAD	1 LARGE CAN CRUSHED PINEAPPLE
2 EGGS, BEAT SLIGHTLY	OR 2 C CHOPPED FRESH PINEAPPLE

PLACE CUBED BREAD IN A BAKING DISH. POUR MELTED BUTTER
OVER THE BREAD. MIX EGGS, SUGAR AND PINEAPPLE AND ADD TO
BREAD CUBES. BAKE AT 350° FOR 25-30 MINUTES.

SOUPS

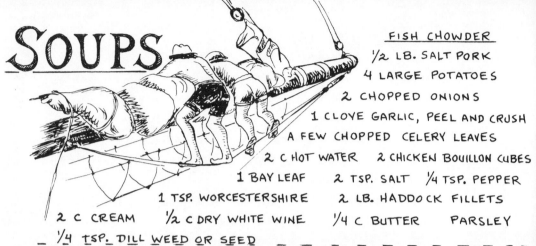

FISH CHOWDER

½ LB. SALT PORK
4 LARGE POTATOES
2 CHOPPED ONIONS
1 CLOVE GARLIC, PEEL AND CRUSH
A FEW CHOPPED CELERY LEAVES
2 C HOT WATER   2 CHICKEN BOUILLON CUBES
1 BAY LEAF   2 TSP. SALT   ¼ TSP. PEPPER
1 TSP. WORCESTERSHIRE   2 LB. HADDOCK FILLETS
2 C CREAM   ½ C DRY WHITE WINE   ¼ C BUTTER   PARSLEY
¼ TSP. DILL WEED OR SEED

FRY UP SALT PORK IN A SOUP POT (OR A FEW SLICES OF CHOPPED BACON).
ADD POTATOES, PEELED AND CUBED, AND ONE CLOVE GARLIC. FRY UP FIVE
MINUTES OR SO AND COVER WITH HOT WATER. ADD CHICKEN BOUILLON
AND CELERY LEAVES. SIMMER UNTIL POTATOES ARE TENDER. THEN
ADD BAY, SALT, PEPPER, DILL, WORCESTERSHIRE. BREAK UP FISH,
DROP IN AND SIMMER FIVE MINUTES. ADD CREAM, WINE AND BUTTER.
GARNISH WITH CHOPPED PARSLEY TO SERVE. FOR A THICKER SOUP,
SPRINKLE IN A LITTLE INSTANT MASHED POTATO.   SERVES 8-10

Clam Chowder

SHUCK 1 QT. CLAMS. WASH AND DRAIN MEAT (SAVE LIQUID). CUT HARD PART
OF CLAM AWAY FROM THE SOFT. CHOP HARD PART. SAUTÉ A 2" CUBE OF SALT
PORK (CUT UP) OR 3 SLICES CHOPPED BACON WITH 1 CHOPPED LARGE
ONION AND THE HARD PART OF CLAMS. (5 MINUTES) STIR IN 3 TBLSP.
FLOUR AND RESERVED CLAM JUICE. ADD 2 C RAW DICED POTATOES
AND HALF A CRUMBLED BAY LEAF. SIMMER UNTIL THE POTATOES
ARE TENDER. ADD SOFT PART OF CLAMS, 3 C HOT MILK, AND 3
TBLSP. BUTTER. DON'T BOIL. SEASON
TO TASTE.

122

Lobster Bisque (SERVES 6)

MEAT FROM 2 MEDIUM LOBSTERS. DICE MEAT AND RESERVE. CRUSH
SHELLS. ADD TO THEM THE TOUGH END OF CLAWS, 2 1/2 C CHICKEN STOCK
AND/OR CLAM JUICE, 1 SLICED ONION, 2 CELERY STALKS AND LEAVES,
1/4 C CHOPPED CARROTS, 2 WHOLE CLOVES, 1 BAY LEAF AND A FEW
PEPPERCORNS. SIMMER 1/2 HOUR AND STRAIN. IF THERE'S CORAL
ROE, SIEVE IT AND MASH IT WITH 1/4 C BUTTER AND WORK IN 1/4 C
FLOUR. POUR 3 C HEATED MILK SLOWLY ON IT AND STIR UNTIL MIXTURE
IS SMOOTH. IF NO ROE, MELT 1/4 C BUTTER AND STIR IN 1/4 C FLOUR AND
GRADUALLY ADD 3 C MILK. HEAT UNTIL THICKENED. ADD 1/4 TSP. NUTMEG.
ADD LOBSTER MEAT AND STOCK AND SIMMER FIVE MINUTES. REMOVE
FROM HEAT AND STIR IN 1 C HOT (NOT BOILING) CREAM. SEASON
WITH THYME, A TOUCH OF CAYENNE AND SHERRY (OPTIONAL).
GARNISH WITH PARSLEY AND PAPRIKA.

CORN CHOWDER (2 QT)

1/2 LB. SALT PORK, DICED	3 C DICED RAW POTATOES
2 MEDIUM ONIONS, CHOPPED	1 CAN CREAM CORN
1/2 C CHOPPED CELERY AND TOPS	2 C EVAPORATED MILK
1/2 BAY LEAF SALT AND PEPPER	1 TBLSP. WORCESTERSHIRE
2 TBLSP. FLOUR	3 CHICKEN BOUILLON CUBES
1 QT. WATER _ 1/4 C BUTTER _ PARSLEY _ _ PAPRIKA _ _	

FRY UP PORK WITH ONION, CELERY AND BAY. REMOVE PORK. BLEND IN
FLOUR – ADD 1 QT. WATER, BOUILLON AND POTATOES. SIMMER 15
MINUTES. ADD CORN AND MILK. HEAT AND ADD SALT, PEPPER, BUTTER
AND WORCESTERSHIRE. GARNISH WITH PARSLEY AND PAPRIKA.

HADDOCK

123

Tomato Bisque   (2 QT.)

MAKE 1 QT. MEDIUM WHITE SAUCE, WITH ½ TSP. OF DRY MUSTARD ADDED. IN A SEPARATE PAN, HEAT 1 CAN (#303) PEELED TOMATOES AND 1 CAN (#303) STEWED TOMATOES. WHEN TOMATOES AND WHITE SAUCE ARE BOTH HOT, ADD ½ TSP. BAKING SODA TO TOMATOES AND STIR UNTIL FROTH SUBSIDES. QUICKLY BLEND WHITE SAUCE AND TOMATOES. SEASON WITH 2 TBLSP. PARMESAN CHEESE, ½ TSP. SWEET BASIL AND 2 TBLSP. BUTTER. GARNISH WITH PARSLEY.

HEARTY SPLIT PEA SOUP   (SERVES 10)

1 HAM BONE AND ANY HAM SCRAPS   SALT AND PEPPER TO TASTE
1 PKG. (1 LB.) DRIED SPLIT PEAS   2 TSP. WORCESTERSHIRE
2 CARROTS, SLICED   ½ BAY LEAF   ¼ TSP. CELERY SALT
2 ONIONS, CHOPPED   ¼ TSP. ONION SALT   ¼ TSP. GARLIC PWD.
7 C WATER   ½ C CHOPPED CELERY LEAVES
¼ TSP. ALLSPICE   ¼ TSP. SEASON-ALL   DASH A-1 SAUCE

IN A KETTLE, HEAT BONE, PEAS, CARROTS, ONIONS AND CELERY LEAVES WITH WATER. BRING TO A BOIL AND ADD SEASONINGS. REDUCE HEAT, COVER AND SIMMER 45 MINUTES, OR UNTIL PEAS ARE TENDER. REMOVE ANY MEAT FROM BONE AND RETURN TO SOUP. DISCARD BONE. ADD MORE WATER IF NEEDED. ADJUST SEASONING.

LENTIL SOUP

1 - 1 LB. PKG. LENTILS   1 C SLICED CELERY   1 LG. PARED POTATO
¼ LB. BACON, DICED   8 OZ. STEWED TOMATOES   1 HAM BONE — OR
2 SLICED ONIONS   SALT, PEPPER TO TASTE   POLISH SAUSAGE
2 DICED CARROTS   ½ TSP. THYME   1 TBLSP. LEMON JCE.
1½ QT. WATER   2 BAY LEAVES   PARSLEY

SAUTE BACON, ONIONS AND CARROTS. ADD LENTILS, WATER, CELERY, TOMATOES, SALT, PEPPER, THYME, AND BAY. WITH MEDIUM GRATER,

GRATE IN POTATO. ADD HAM BONE. SIMMER, COVERED, 1 1/2 HR.
REMOVE BAY LEAVES AND BONE, LEAVING IN ANY HAM SCRAPS. IF
USING POLISH SAUSAGE, ADD IT NOW. HEAT AND ADJUST SEASONING.
ADD LEMON JUICE JUST BEFORE SERVING. GARNISH WITH PARSLEY.

PUMPKIN SOUP (SERVES 8-10)

YOU MAY USE PUMPKIN, BUTTERNUT OR HUBBARD SQUASH. PEEL
2 1/2 LB. PUMPKIN OR SQUASH. SCRAPE OUT THE SEEDS, CUT IN
CHUNKS AND BOIL IN SALTED WATER UNTIL TENDER. DRAIN,
RESERVING WATER AND MASH THE PUMPKIN FINELY. ADD PUMPKIN
WATER (OR CHICKEN BROTH) UNTIL IT'S A THICK PURÉE. ADD 2
CHOPPED CARROTS, 1 DICED STALK CELERY, 3 SLICES CHOPPED
BACON, 1 LARGE CHOPPED ONION, AND 1 CHOPPED GREEN PEPPER.
SIMMER UNTIL VEGETABLES ARE TENDER. ADD 1 TBLSP. FLOUR
(MIXED TO A PASTE WITH WATER), 1/2 TSP. THYME, 1 C CANNED
TOMATOES (OR CHOPPED FRESH), SALT AND PEPPER TO TASTE
AND 2 TBLSP. BUTTER. HEAT 1/2 CAN EVAPORATED MILK AND ADD
JUST BEFORE SERVING. GARNISH WITH FRESH CHOPPED PARSLEY.

MINESTRONE — A GREAT SOUP FOR LUNCH ON A COOL DAY. IN-

GREDIENT AMOUNTS ARE FLEXIBLE, UTILIZING LEFT-OVERS. I USUALLY
FRY UP 3 CHOPPED SLICES BACON WITH 2 CHOPPED ONIONS, 1 CLOVE
MINCED GARLIC, 2 CHOPPED POTATOES, 2 CHOPPED CARROTS AND
1/2 C DICED CELERY (FEW LEAVES TOO). ADD 1/4 C OLIVE OIL, 2 TSP.
BASIL, 2 TBLSP. PARSLEY, 1/2 TSP. OREGANO, 1 C CHOPPED CABBAGE
AND 1 C TOMATOES. ZUCCHINI MAY BE ADDED — EVEN
EGGPLANT. ADD CONSOMME OR BEEF STOCK,
AND BEANS. (USE DRIED WHITE BEANS
THAT HAVE BEEN SOAKED AND COOKED, OR
CANNED — WE'VE EVEN USED LEFT-OVERS
FROM THE BEAN POTS). TOSS IN A HAND-
FUL OF MACARONI. SIMMER 10 MINUTES.
TOP WITH PARMESAN AND PARSLEY.

CHILI (FOR 10)

SOAK ½ PKG. RED KIDNEY BEANS OVERNIGHT. CHANGE THE WATER AND CHOP IN AN ONION AND ADD 1 MASHED CLOVE GARLIC. BRING TO A BOIL AND SIMMER UNTIL TENDER. DO NOT ADD SALT AT THIS TIME AS IT TOUGHENS THE BEANS. — OR YOU MAY USE A 20-OZ. CAN OF KIDNEY BEANS.   SAUTÉ 3 CHOPPED SLICES BACON WITH 1 CHOPPED ONION, 1 CRUSHED CLOVE GARLIC AND 1 LB. GROUND BEEF UNTIL BEEF IS BROWN. ADD 1 TBLSP. CHILI PWD., ½ TSP. CELERY SEED, ½ TSP. SEASON-ALL, AND SALT AND BLACK PEPPER TO TASTE. ADD 1 CAN (#2½) TOMATOES, 1 TBLSP. WORCESTERSHIRE AND 1 TBLSP. BUTTER. SIMMER 30 MINUTES AND ADD THE BEANS. SERVE WITH STEAMED RICE.

MEXICALI BAKE (SERVES 10)

1 LB. NOODLES	1 CHOPPED GREEN PEPPER	1 TBLSP. CHILI PWD.
5 SLICES BACON	1 TBLSP. OREGANO	SALT AND PEPPER
2 LB. HAMBURGER	1 LARGE CAN TOMATOES	1 TBLSP. WORCESTERSHIRE
2 CHOPPED ONIONS	1-8 OZ CAN TOMATO SAUCE	1 TBLSP. PARSLEY
2 CLOVES GARLIC, MINCED	1 CAN NIBLET CORN	½ LB. GRATED AMERICAN CHEESE

BROWN BACON (CHOPPED) AND ADD MEAT, ONIONS, GARLIC, GREEN PEPPER AND OREGANO. SIMMER UNTIL MEAT IS BROWN. ADD TOMATOES, TOMATO SAUCE AND CORN. ADD SALT AND PEPPER TO TASTE, CHILI PWD., WORCESTERSHIRE AND PARSLEY. SIMMER ONE HOUR. CHECK SEASONING. ADD COOKED NOODLES AND SPRINKLE CHEESE ON TOP. SERVE WITH HOT FRENCH BREAD.

Spaghetti Sauce

SAUTÉ IN 3 TBLSP. OLIVE OIL — 1 C MINCED ONIONS, 1 MINCED CLOVE GARLIC, 1 TSP. OREGANO AND 1 LB. HAMBURGER. WHEN HAMBURGER IS BROWN, ADD 1 CAN (1 LB. 13 OZ.) ITALIAN PEELED TOMATOES, 2 8 OZ. CANS TOMATO SAUCE, 1 TSP. SALT, 1/4 TSP. PEPPER, 1 TSP. ONION SALT, 1 TSP. BASIL, 1 TBLSP. WORCESTERSHIRE AND 1 TSP. SUGAR. SIMMER ABOUT 1 HOUR. I LIKE TO STIR IN 1/4 C RED WINE.

IF TIME IS SHORT AND THE STOVE TOP IS IN DEMAND, A PKG. SPAGHETTI SAUCE IS USED, ADDING ONION, GARLIC AND THE GROUND BEEF.

Lasagna notes — A TROUBLE-SAVER (GLEANED FROM "HARVEY GAMAGE") — IT IS <u>NOT</u> NECESSARY TO BOIL THE PASTA BEFORE YOU LAY IT UP IN THE PANS WITH THE CHEESES AND THE SAUCE. TRY IT — YOU'LL LIKE IT! AND IF THE GROCER HAS NO RICOTTA, USE COTTAGE CHEESE, ADDING 1 TSP. SUGAR TO A PINT.

拓 STIR FRIED RICE 本 (FOR 6)

3 C COLD COOKED RICE	2 CELERY STALKS, SLICED
2 C SLIVERED MEAT (MAY BE STEAK, CHICKEN, VEAL OR A COMBINATION)	
3 SLICES BACON, CHOPPED	1 CAN WATER CHESTNUTS, CHOP
3 EGGS	1 C BEAN SPROUTS
2 ONIONS, COARSELY CHOPPED	SOY SAUCE
1 GREEN PEPPER, COARSELY CHOPPED	CHINESE NOODLES
1 MINCED CLOVE GARLIC	SWEET AND SOUR SAUCE

MARINATE MEAT IN TERIYAKI OR SOY SAUCE 1/2 HR. SAUTÉ ONIONS, PEPPERS, CELERY AND GARLIC IN 2 TBLSP. OIL 5 MINUTES. SET ASIDE. SAUTÉ MEAT WITH BACON A FEW MINUTES. ADD TO VEGETABLES. SCRAMBLE EGGS IN OIL UNTIL HARD. SLIVER AND ADD TO MEAT. STIR-FRY RICE IN HOT OIL, ADDING SOY SAUCE AS YOU DO (ABOUT 1/4 C). MIX ALL BUT CHINESE NOODLES AND SWEET AND SOUR, WHICH ARE SERVED AT TABLE AS TOPPINGS.

127

Red Flannel Hash   (Serves 6)

1 ½ c chopped corned beef
1 ½ c chopped boiled potatoes
1 ½ c chopped boiled beets
1 medium onion, minced

¼ c milk
salt and pepper to taste
1 tsp. Worcestershire
2 tblsp. butter

Add all ingredients to the butter in a hot frying pan. Stir until heated. Cook until the mixture is brown and crusty underneath. Fold as an omelet. Garnish with parsley.

Pizza   (2 - 12" pizzas)

Dough: 1 c warm water   2 tblsp. shortening   4 c flour
1 pkg. dry yeast   ¼ tsp. salt   2 tsp. oil

Dissolve yeast in warm water. Add shortening, salt and half of flour. Gradually add the rest of the flour and turn out on a floured board to knead until smooth. Place in an oiled bowl, turn dough to coat, cover and let rise until double. Punch down and knead a few minutes. Roll into 2 circles (or to fit your pans). Fit into pans leaving an edge up the sides. Fill as desired.

Pizza Sauce

In 1 tblsp. oil, saute ¼ c chopped onion and 1 minced clove garlic until soft. Add 1 can (1 lb. 3 oz.) whole tomatoes (mash tomatoes with a fork), 1-8 oz. can tomato sauce, 1 bay leaf, 1 tsp. salt, 1 tsp. sugar, 1 tsp. oregano and ¼ tsp. pepper. Simmer 30 minutes.   Spread on pizza dough.

Filling variations: Anchovy - arrange anchovies (2 oz. can) on sauce. Cover with 1 lb. sliced mozzarella cheese.

Sausage: Place browned, drained sausage on sauce and cover with 1 lb. sliced mozzarella cheese.

Onion - Green Pepper: Slice 2 onions and 1 green pepper thinly - spread on sauce and cover with 1 c parmesan cheese - or mozzarella.

Sliced salami is good and mushrooms go with anything.

Oven 450°. Bake 25 minutes.

128

TURKEY OR CHICKEN LOAF (MAKES 1 LOAF)

2 C DICED OR GROUND COOKED CHICKEN OR TURKEY

2 C SOFT BREAD CRUMBS   1 TBLSP. MINCED PARSLEY

1/4 C CHOPPED ONION   1/2 TSP. SALT   1/4 TSP. PAPRIKA

2 TBLSP. CHOPPED PIMIENTO   3 EGGS, BEATEN   2 C MILK

1/2 C CHOPPED CELERY   2 TBLSP. BUTTER

COMBINE ALL THE INGREDIENTS AND MIX WELL. YOU MAY ADD 1/2 C
MUSHROOMS OR SERVE WITH MUSHROOM SOUP AS A SAUCE. POUR
INTO A GREASED 9 x 5" LOAF PAN. BAKE AT 350° ABOUT 40
MINUTES. SERVE WITH MUSHROOM, CHEESE OR EGG SAUCE.

PINEAPPLE - GLAZED HAM LOAF

1 TBLSP. BUTTER   MILK   1 TBLSP. CHOPPED PARSLEY

1/3 C BROWN SUGAR   1 EGG, BEAT   1 TBLSP. GRATED ONION

1/2 TSP. GROUND CLOVES   1 C PEPPERIDGE FARM STUFFING MIX

1 CAN (13 1/2 OZ.) CRUSHED PINEAPPLE   1/4 C CHOPPED GREEN PEPPER

1 LB. COOKED, GROUND HAM   1 LB. HAMBURGER   1 TBLSP. MUSTARD

MELT BUTTER IN A 9 x 5" LOAF PAN. MIX BROWN SUGAR AND CLOVES AND
SPRINKLE INTO PAN. DRAIN PINEAPPLE (SAVE JUICE) AND SPREAD ON SUGAR.
IN BOWL, COMBINE REMAINING INGREDIENTS, USING PINEAPPLE JUICE
AND ENOUGH MILK TO MAKE 1 C. TURN MEAT MIX INTO PAN, PRESSING
FIRMLY. BAKE AT 350° 1 1/4 HOURS. DRAIN ANY LIQUID AND INVERT
ON A PLATTER TO SERVE.

MEAT LOAF

2 LB. HAMBURGER   1 C TOMATO JUICE   SALT AND PEPPER

3 SLICES BREAD, CRUMBED   1/4 C CATSUP   TO TASTE

1/2 C MILK   1 TBLSP. WORCESTERSHIRE   1/2 C CHOPPED

1 TBLSP. PARSLEY   1 CHOPPED ONION   GREEN PEPPER

1 PKG. LIPTONS DRY ONION SOUP   1 EGG   1/2 TSP. SEASON - ALL

MIX ALL TOGETHER AND PACK IN A 9 x 5" LOAF PAN. BAKE AT 350°
1 HOUR COVERED WITH FOIL AND 1/2 HOUR UNCOVERED. TOP WITH
CHEESE, TOMATOES, SWEET AND SOUR — WHATEVER YOU WISH!

★ MEATS FOWL FISH

THERE ARE WONDERFUL MEATS TO WORK WITH ON "ADVENTURE". PURCHASED FROM A HOTEL SUPPLY CHAIN, THE TURKEY, LAMB, PORK AND BEEF ARE BONED, NETTED, AND EVEN HAVE SELF-TIMERS BUILT IN. IT'S HARD TO GO WRONG!

TURKEY - IS PRE-COOKED TURKEY BREAST WHICH NEEDS ONLY TO BE BRUSHED WITH BUTTER AND BAKED UNTIL GOOD AND HOT.

LAMB IS BEST WITH SLIVERS OF GARLIC BURIED INSIDE, BRUSHED WITH A MIXTURE OF WORCESTERSHIRE AND LEMON JUICE. SEASON WITH SALT, PEPPER, BASIL, MARJORAM, THYME AND ONION.

PORK IS NICE WITH THE FOLLOWING SAUCE TO BASTE WITH AS IT ROASTS: 1/2 C MADEIRA WINE, 1 TSP. SALT, DASH PEPPER, AND 1/8 TSP. GROUND NUTMEG. BRUSH MEAT OFTEN. THE GRAVY MADE FROM THESE PAN DRIPPINGS IS SOMETHING SPECIAL.

BEEF: BRUSH WITH WORCESTERSHIRE AND SEASON WITH SALT, PEPPER, CELERY SEED, SEASON-ALL AND ROSEMARY. I LIKE TO CHOP AN ONION INTO THE PAN TOWARDS THE END OF THE ROASTING.

FISH: FRESH HADDOCK IS SO GOOD! BRUSHED WITH LEMON BUTTER, SPRINKLED WITH PAPRIKA AND BAKED AT 350° ABOUT 20 MINUTES UNTIL IT FLAKES EASILY WITH A FORK. FOOD FIT FOR THE GODS! HERE ARE A FEW WAYS WITH FISH THAT WE'RE FOND OF:

(OVEN – 350°)   FISH FLORENTINE   (SERVES 6)

3 C COOKED FISH	1/3 C BUTTER	3 SHAKES TABASCO
3 C MILK DASH OF WINE	1 TSP. SALT	1 C GRATED CHEDDAR CHEESE
1/3 C FLOUR	1 TSP. MUSTARD	2 PKG. DRAINED SPINACH

MAKE A SAUCE WITH BUTTER, FLOUR, MILK, MUSTARD, SALT, TABASCO AND WINE. PLACE SPINACH IN A CASSEROLE, THEN FISH. POUR SAUCE OVER, SPRINKLE WITH SLIVERED ALMONDS, TOP WITH CHEESE AND BAKE 30 MINUTES.

130

Beth's "Ah So" Fish (for 6)

BAKE 2 LB. FISH FILLETS (SEE PAGE 130) AND
SERVE WITH THE FOLLOWING SAUCE POURED OVER
THE FISH AND CHINESE NOODLES HEAPED AROUND THE EDGES.
 SAUCE: SAUTÉ 1/2 C MUSHROOM PIECES, 1/3 C CHOPPED ONIONS, 1/4 C
EACH CHOPPED GREEN AND RED PEPPERS (IF RED PEPPERS ARE NOT
AVAILABLE, CHOPPED RED PIMIENTOS MAY BE ADDED TO SAUCE LATER)
ADD 1 CAN CREAM OF MUSHROOM SOUP, 1/2 CAN MILK, 1/4 C SHERRY.
SEASON TO TASTE WITH SALT, PEPPER AND GARLIC.

MACADAMIA NUT FISH (SERVES 6)

BAKE OR SAUTÉ 2 LB. FISH FILLETS. POUR THE FOLLOWING SAUCE
OVER FISH TO SERVE, SPRINKLED WITH PARSLEY.
 SAUCE: MIX 2 TSP. CORNSTARCH IN 2 TBLSP. WATER. ADD TO 1 C RICH
CHICKEN BROTH, ADD THE JUICE FROM 1/2 LEMON, 1/4 C HOLLANDAISE
AND 1/2 C CRUSHED MACADAMIA NUTS.

OVEN FRIED FISH (SERVES 6)

2 LB. FISH FILLETS	1/4 TSP. TARRAGON	1 TSP. WORCESTERSHIRE
1/4 C EVAPORATED MILK	1/4 TSP. DILL WEED	1/4 C BUTTER
1 TSP. SALT	1/2 C PROGRESSO SEASONED BREAD CRUMBS	

MIX MILK, SALT, TARRAGON, DILL AND WORCESTERSHIRE IN A FLAT DISH.
PLACE CRUMBS IN ANOTHER. DIP FISH IN MILK, THEN ROLL IN CRUMBS.
PLACE FILLETS IN AN OILED SHALLOW PAN IN A SINGLE LAYER. DRIZZLE
MELTED BUTTER OVER FISH. BAKE AT 500° 20 MINUTES UNTIL GOLDEN
AND EASILY FLAKED. SERVE WITH MUSTARD SAUCE: SAUTE IN 1/3 C BUTTER,
1/3 C MINCED ONION AND 1 MINCED CLOVE GARLIC. WHEN ONION IS TENDER,
ADD 1/2 TSP. SALT, DASH PEPPER, 2 TSP. WORCESTERSHIRE, 1 1/2 TSP.
PREPARED MUSTARD AND 3 TBLSP. CHILI SAUCE. HEAT.

BAKED STUFFED HADDOCK   (SERVES 6)

MAKE UP A VEGETABLE STUFFING. SAUTÉ IN 3 TBLSP. BUTTER — 1/2 C ONION (CHOPPED), 1/4 C CHOPPED CELERY, 1/4 C CHOPPED GREEN PEPPER, AND 1/2 C CHOPPED MUSHROOMS. STIR IN 2 C SOFT BREAD CRUMBS, 1 TSP. SALT, DASH OF PEPPER, 1/4 TSP. TARRAGON AND 1/4 TSP. DILL WEED. PLACE 2 LBS. OF HADDOCK FILLETS IN A LAYER IN A BUTTERED SHALLOW PAN. SPRINKLE WITH LEMON JUICE. SPREAD STUFFING OVER FISH AND COVER WITH PEELED, SLICED TOMATOES. BAKE AT 375° ABOUT 40 MINUTES.

CHICKEN WAYS:

OVEN FRIED: COAT CHICKEN BREASTS AND THIGHS WITH EITHER EVAPORATED MILK OR FRENCH DRESSING. ROLL IN SEASONED CORN FLAKE CRUMBS AND BAKE AT 350° FOR 1 - 1 1/2 HOURS.

SHERRIED CHICKEN: BAKE CHICKEN PARTS IN A 350° OVEN ONE HOUR AND THEN POUR OVER A MIXTURE OF 1 CAN CREAM OF MUSHROOM SOUP AND 1/2 C SHERRY. BAKE ONE HOUR MORE.

COUNTRY CHICKEN

COAT CHICKEN PARTS IN SEASONED FLOUR AND SAUTÉ IN BACON GREASE UNTIL BROWN. PLACE IN A CASSEROLE. IN 3 TBLSP. BUTTER, SAUTÉ 1 ONION, COARSELY CUT, AND 1 GREEN PEPPER, COARSELY CUT. ADD 3 TBLSP. CURRY PWD. AND LET COOK UP A MINUTE. ADD 1 LARGE CAN (#2 1/2) TOMATOES. POUR OVER CHICKEN. ADD 1/2 C RAISINS AND BAKE AT 350° ONE HOUR.

MANDARIN CHICKEN

1 TO 3 CHICKENS, QUARTERED	2 TBLSP. SOY	2 TBLSP. SUGAR
1 CAN MANDARIN ORANGES	1 C TOMATO SAUCE	PINEAPPLE CHUNKS
1/3 C VINEGAR	1 CLOVE GARLIC, MASHED	GREEN PEPPER
2 TBLSP. BUTTER	1/2 TSP. GINGER	SQUARES

BAKE CHICKEN AT 350°. BRUSH WITH BUTTER AND BASTE WITH THE FOLLOWING SAUCE: MIX MANDARIN JUICE, TOMATO SAUCE, VINEGAR, BUTTER, SOY, GARLIC, AND GINGER. BRING TO A BOIL. BEFORE SERVING, ADD SUGAR, ORANGES, PINEAPPLE AND PEPPERS. ADD DRIPPINGS FROM CHICKEN. STIR AND POUR OVER CHICKEN PARTS.

132

ham

THE HAMS WORKED WITH ARE BONELESS AND PRE-COOKED — ALL READY
FOR GLAZING. SCORE HAM 1/8" DEEP IN DIAGONAL CUTS, STUD WITH
CLOVES AND BRUSH WITH A GLAZE.

ORANGE GLAZE: MIX 1/2 C STRAINED ORANGE MARMALADE WITH
1 C DARK CORN SYRUP AND 2 TSP. DRY MUSTARD.

MAPLE: MIX 3/4 C MAPLE SYRUP WITH 3/4 C DARK CORN SYRUP AND
2 TBLSP. PREPARED MUSTARD.

CRUST: MIX 1 1/3 C BROWN SUGAR, 2 TSP. DRY MUSTARD, 1/3 C
FINE DRY BREAD CRUMBS AND 3 TBLSP. RED WINE OR CIDAR VINEGAR.
PAT THIS MIXTURE ON HAM AND THEN STUD WITH CLOVES.

BAKE HAM AT 375° UNTIL BROWNED AND HOT THROUGH.
SLICE AND SERVE WITH RAISIN SAUCE OR FRUIT COMPOTE.

RAISIN SAUCE

IN A SAUCEPAN, MIX 1/4 C BROWN SUGAR, 1 1/2 TBLSP. CORN STARCH,
1/8 TSP. SALT AND 1 C CIDER OR BEER. STIR IN 1/4 C RAISINS, 1/4
TSP. CLOVES AND 1/2 TSP. CINNAMON. COOK AND STIR UNTIL THICK
AND CLEAR. ADD 1 TBLSP. BUTTER.

Fruit COMPOTE

SLICE UP IN A PAN: 8 SMALL PEACHES,
APPLES OR PEARS (OR A COMBINATION)
ADD:

2/3 C RED WINE	1/8 TSP. SALT
2/3 C SUGAR	4 WHOLE CLOVES
1/2 STICK CINNAMON	1/2 THIN SLICED LEMON

BRING TO A BOIL, LOWER THE HEAT AND SIMMER
15 MINUTES. YOU MAY VARY THE FRUIT —
USING DRIED, FRESH OR CANNED.

Corned Beef

COVER A 5 LB. PIECE OF CORNED BEEF WITH BOILING WATER. ADD
1 MASHED CLOVE GARLIC, 1 QUARTERED ONION, 2 BAY LEAVES, 2
WHOLE CLOVES, 10 BLACK PEPPERCORNS AND 1/4 TSP. MUSTARD SEED.
SIMMER 4 HOURS. SERVE WITH:

HORSERADISH SAUCE

1 C CREAM SAUCE	2 TBLSP. WHIPPING CREAM	1 TBLSP. VINEGAR
3 TBLSP. HORSERADISH	1 TSP. SUGAR	1 TSP. DRY MUSTARD

MIX ALL TOGETHER AND BRING TO A BOIL.

New England Boiled Dinner

AFTER CORNED BEEF HAS SIMMERED IN THE STOCK 4 HOURS,
REMOVE MEAT AND ADD THE FOLLOWING TO THE BROTH:

3 SMALL PARSNIPS	3 LARGE YELLOW TURNIPS
6 LARGE CARROTS	8 SMALL ONIONS

SIMMER 15 MINUTES AND ADD 6 MEDIUM POTATOES, QUARTERED.
SIMMER 15 MINUTES MORE AND ADD A HEAD OF CABBAGE, CUT
INTO WEDGES. TEN MINUTES FOR THE CABBAGE. REHEAT THE
MEAT IN THE STOCK AND SERVE WITH THE VEGETABLES HEAPED
AROUND THE CORNED BEEF.

I ALMOST FORGOT—

Yorkshire Pudding (SERVE WITH ROAST BEEF)

HAVE ALL INGREDIENTS AT ROOM TEMPERATURE. SIFT 1 C FLOUR WITH
1/2 TSP. SALT. MAKE A WELL AND POUR IN 1/2 C MILK. STIR IN. BEAT
2 EGGS UNTIL FLUFFY AND MIX IN. ADD 1/2 C MILK. BEAT WELL UNTIL
LARGE BUBBLES RISE. THIS MAY NOW STAND IN THE REFRIGERATOR
FOR AN HOUR, COVERED. BEAT AGAIN. IN A 9 X 12" OVENPROOF
DISH, MELT BEEF DRIPPINGS (1/4"). PAN SHOULD BE SMOKING
HOT (MUFFIN TINS CAN BE USED). POUR IN BATTER. BAKE
AT 400° 20 MINUTES, AND AT 350° FOR 10-15
MINUTES LONGER. SERVE IMMEDIATELY. IF IT BAKES
UNDER THE ROAST AND DRIPPINGS FALL ON THE BATTER,
IT'S DELICIOUS!

134

Meat Notes

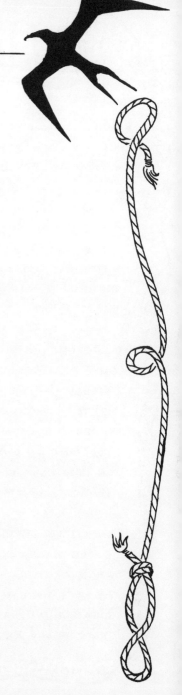

VEGETABLES

ARTICHOKES

CANNED ARTICHOKE HEARTS GIVE AN ELEGANT TOUCH TO SALADS, BUT THEY ARE ALSO A FINE ACCOMPANIMENT TO A MEAT COURSE WHEN SERVED AS FOLLOWS:

Artichoke Parmesan Casserole (SERVES 6)

2 CANS ARTICHOKE HEARTS, DRAINED   PARMESAN CHEESE

PROGRESSO SEASONED_ BREAD CRUMBS _ _SALAD_OIL _ _ _

RINSE ARTICHOKE HEARTS, DRAIN AND CUT IN QUARTERS. SPRINKLE WITH OLIVE OIL AND PARMESAN CHEESE. COVER WITH BREAD CRUMBS STIRRED IN MELTED BUTTER. BAKE 30 MINUTES AT 350°.

GREEN BEANS

I PREFER TO UNDERCOOK FRESH VEGETABLES, AS THE FLAVOR AND COLOR ARE SO MUCH NICER. GREEN BEANS LEND THEMSELVES TO ENDLESS VARIATIONS. ① COOK WITH ONION AND BACON PIECES OR HAM BITS.

② TOP COOKED BEANS WITH CREAM OF MUSHROOM SOUP AND COVER WITH CANNED FRENCH FRIED ONION RINGS.

③ SAUTÉ ¼ C SLIVERED ALMONDS IN ¼ C BUTTER UNTIL BROWN AND STIR INTO COOKED BEANS. SALT AND PEPPER TO TASTE.

④ ADD CHOPPED MUSHROOMS AND/OR WATER CHESTNUTS. SEASON TO TASTE.

SWEET SOUR BEANS

COOK 1 LB. GREEN BEANS UNTIL BARELY TENDER. FRY UP 3 CHOPPED SLICES BACON AND 2 TBLSP. CHOPPED ONION. REMOVE BACON WHEN CRISP AND ADD TO PAN 1 TBLSP. WINE VINEGAR, 1 TBLSP. SUGAR AND ½ TSP. SALT. POUR OVER BEANS AND ADD BACON.

MAINE BAKED BEANS

1 LB. JACOB CATTLE BEANS (OR YELLOW, PEA OR KIDNEY)

1/4 LB. SALT PORK   1/3 C MOLASSES   1/3 C CATSUP

1 MEDIUM ONION   2 TSP. SALT   1/4 TSP. PEPPER

2 TBLSP. BROWN SUGAR   1 TSP. DRY MUSTARD   1 C HOT WATER

1 TBLSP. WORCESTERSHIRE   1/2 TSP. GARLIC PWD.

YOU MAY USE PART MAPLE SYRUP FOR THE MOLASSES. SOAK THE
BEANS OVERNIGHT IN WATER TO COVER. THEN PARBOIL UNTIL THE SKINS
CRACK WHEN BLOWN UPON. (1/2 - 1 HOUR) QUARTER THE ONION AND
PUT IN THE BOTTOM OF THE BEAN POT. ADD THE BEANS. CUT THROUGH
RIND OF THE SALT PORK AND PLACE ON TOP OF BEANS. MIX REMAINING
INGREDIENTS AND POUR OVER BEANS. BAKE AT 300° - 4 TO 6
HOURS. ADD WATER IF NECESSARY. —THE WOOD STOVE IS PERFECT
FOR THIS DISH... EITHER IN THE BOTTOM OF THE OVEN OR ON THE BACK
OF THE STOVE.

BEETS

① SEASON BEETS WITH SALT, PEPPER, PARSLEY AND BUTTER.

② SEASON WITH BUTTER, BROWN SUGAR AND GRATED ORANGE RIND.

BEETS AND SOUR CREAM

COMBINE AND HEAT TOGETHER }

3 C COOKED SLICED BEETS   SALT AND PEPPER

1/2 C SOUR CREAM   1 TBLSP. HORSERADISH

1 TBLSP. CHOPPED CHIVES   1 TBLSP. PARSLEY

HARVARD BEETS

3 C COOKED, SLICED BEETS   1/4 TSP. PEPPER

1/2 C SUGAR   1/4 TSP. CLOVES   1/2 C CIDAR VINEGAR

1/2 TSP. SALT   1 TBLSP. CORNSTARCH   2 TBLSP. BUTTER

STIR TOGETHER IN A SAUCEPAN — SUGAR, CORNSTARCH, SALT,
CLOVES AND VINEGAR. COOK AND STIR UNTIL MIXTURE IS
THICK AND CLEAR. ADD BEETS AND BUTTER. THE ADDITION
OF A COUPLE OF TBLSP. OF ORANGE MARMALADE IS
INTERESTING.

Broccoli and Brussels Sprouts

WE TREAT BOTH OF THESE VEGETABLES MUCH THE SAME. COOKED ONLY UNTIL TENDER-CRISP, SIMPLY ADD SALT, PEPPER, BUTTER AND A SQUEEZE OF LEMON JUICE. SOMETIMES THEY'RE SERVED WITH A CHEESE OR HOLLANDAISE SAUCE.

BRUSSELS SPROUTS MAY BE VARIED BY MIXING IN CHESTNUTS OR WALNUTS AND TOPPING WITH BUTTERED BREAD CRUMBS.

JIFFY HOLLANDAISE (1½ c)

HEAT 1 c MAYONNAISE OR SALAD DRESSING IN THE TOP OF A DOUBLE BOILER, STIRRING. REMOVE FROM HEAT AND FOLD IN ¼ c HEAVY CREAM, WHIPPED AND ½ TBLSP. SNIPPED CHIVES. STIR UNTIL BLENDED.

HOLLANDAISE

BEAT WELL 2 EGG YOLKS (OR 1 WHOLE EGG). ADD SALT, PEPPER, ¼ TSP. DRY MUSTARD, DASH OF CAYENNE (OR TABASCO) AND A SQUIRT OF LEMON JUICE. MELT UP ½ LB. BUTTER. TAKE FROM FLAME. ADD A BIT OF BUTTER TO EGG, BEATING WITH A WHISK ALL THE WHILE. BEAT-BEAT AS YOU DRIP IN BUTTER. WHEN IT IS ALL BLENDED, YOU MAY NEED A LITTLE MORE LEMON.

Cabbage

BRAISED WHITE — SAUTÉ 3 BACON SLICES, DRAIN AND CRUMBLE. TOSS 2 LB. FINE SHREDDED CABBAGE IN BACON FAT. ADD 1½ TSP. SALT, DASH PEPPER AND 3 TBLSP. WHITE WINE VINEGAR. COOK 3 MINUTES.

CABBAGE IN MUSTARD SAUCE — SHRED A SMALL HEAD OF CABBAGE. SAUTÉ IT LIGHTLY IN BUTTER OR BACON DRIPPINGS. ADD ½ TSP. SALT, ¼ TSP. PAPRIKA, ½ TSP. CARAWAY SEED, AND 2 TBLSP. MINCED ONION. PLACE IN A GREASED BAKING DISH. POUR OVER 1½ c SOUR CREAM THAT HAS BEEN MIXED WITH 1 TBLSP. MUSTARD. BAKE AT 375° FOR 20 MINUTES. (SERVES 4)

138

RED CABBAGE

2 LB. HEAD RED CABBAGE	1/4 TSP. SALT
4 CHOPPED SLICES BACON	1/2 C RED WINE
1/4 C CHOPPED ONION	1/4 TSP. CARAWAY SEED
2 APPLES	2 TBLSP. HONEY

SAUTÉ BACON AND ONION. ADD SHREDDED CABBAGE, COVER AND COOK TEN MINUTES. ADD APPLES (SLICED), CARAWAY, SALT, WINE AND HONEY. COVER AND SIMMER AN HOUR.

CARROTS

GRATE CARROTS (1 PER PERSON) AND A LITTLE ONION. STIR-FRY QUICKLY IN BUTTER IN A HOT SKILLET. ADD SALT AND PEPPER TO TASTE... NO MORE THAN 3 MINUTES COOKING!

COINTREAU CARROTS

COOK 2 BUNCHES OF SMALL CARROTS IN ORANGE JUICE, 1/4 TSP. SALT AND 6 TBLSP. WATER UNTIL TENDER-CRISP. DRAIN. MELT 1/4 C BUTTER AND ADD 2 TBLSP. SUGAR AND 2 TBLSP. COINTREAU. ADD CARROTS AND COOK UNTIL GLAZED, TURNING. SERVE WITH COCONUT AS A GARNISH IF YOU WISH.

DILL WEED OR SEED IS LOVELY ADDED TO CARROTS WITH SALT, PEPPER AND BUTTER.

GOOD COMBO - CARROTS, MUSHROOMS, CHIVES AND ARTICHOKE HEARTS. SEASON WITH SALT AND PEPPER AND TOP WITH BUTTERED BREAD CRUMBS. BAKE AT 350° FOR 20 MINUTES.

GINGER CARROTS: SAUTÉ CHOPPED ONION IN BUTTER AND ADD TO COOKED, DRAINED CARROTS. ADD BROWN SUGAR, CHOPPED PRESERVED GINGER - HEAT AND STIR IN A COUPLE TBLSP. RUM. CHEERS!

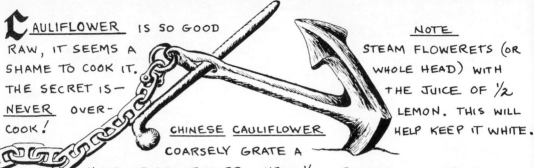

CAULIFLOWER IS SO GOOD
RAW, IT SEEMS A
SHAME TO COOK IT.
THE SECRET IS —
NEVER OVER-
COOK!

NOTE

STEAM FLOWERETS (OR
WHOLE HEAD) WITH
THE JUICE OF ½
LEMON. THIS WILL
HELP KEEP IT WHITE.

CHINESE CAULIFLOWER

COARSELY GRATE A
HEAD OF CAULIFLOWER. HEAT ¼ C BUTTER IN A LARGE
SKILLET, AND QUICKLY SAUTÉ CAULIFLOWER (ABOUT 3 MINUTES).
SEASON WITH SALT, PEPPER AND JUICE FROM ½ A LEMON. TO SERVE,
SPRINKLE WITH PARMESAN CHEESE OR PAPRIKA.

SESAME CAULIFLOWER   (SERVES 6)

COOK CAULIFLOWER (BROKEN UP) UNTIL TENDER-CRISP. (1 HEAD). DRAIN
AND SET ASIDE. IN A SAUCEPAN, TOAST 2 TBLSP. SESAME SEED UNTIL
BROWN, SHAKING PAN. PUT ON PAPER TOWEL. IN SAUCEPAN, MELT
2 TBLSP. BUTTER, STIR IN 2 TBLSP. FLOUR. GRADUALLY STIR IN
1 C CHICKEN BROTH AND COOK, STIRRING, UNTIL THICK. GENTLY
STIR IN 2 TSP. LEMON JUICE, ½ TSP. SALT AND THE CAULIFLOWER.
SPRINKLE WITH SESAME SEED.

WITH ALMONDS : BROWN CHOPPED BLANCHED ALMONDS IN HOT BUTTER. POUR
    OVER COOKED CAULIFLOWER HEAD AND SEASON WITH SALT AND PEPPER.
WITH HOLLANDAISE : SERVE HOT CAULIFLOWER WITH HOLLANDAISE.
WITH CHEESE SAUCE : SERVE HOT CAULIFLOWER WITH A CREAM SAUCE TO
    WHICH YOU HAVE ADDED EITHER GRATED SWISS OR AMERICAN CHEESE.
    GARNISH WITH PARSLEY OR CHIVES OR BUTTERED TOASTED BREAD CRUMBS.

(OVEN 350°)   ## CAULIFLOWER PAPRIKA   (SERVES 6)

PLACE COOKED FLOWERETS FROM 1 HEAD IN A BUTTERED CASSEROLE. SAUTÉ
¼ C CHOPPED GREEN PEPPER IN 2 TBLSP. BUTTER 3 MINUTES. ADD 2 TBLSP.
FLOUR, ½ TSP. SALT AND ½ TSP. PAPRIKA. STIR IN 1 C MILK AND COOK
UNTIL THICK. TAKE FROM FIRE AND ADD 1 C SOUR CREAM. POUR OVER
CAULIFLOWER. CRUMBLE 1 - 3 OZ. PKG, CREAM CHEESE ON SAUCE. BAKE 20
MINUTES.

CORN

FOR FRESH, SWEET CORN, WE LIKE TO POUR BOILING WATER OVER THE EARS, ADD A TSP. OF SUGAR (FOR 6 EARS) AND BOIL THEM FOUR TO TEN MINUTES, DEPENDING ON AGE.

CREAMY FRESH CORN

7 OR 8 EARS CORN   1 TBLSP. SUGAR   1/2 C MILK
1/3 - 1/2 C BUTTER   1 TSP. SEASON SALT   1/2 C LIGHT CREAM
2 TBLSP. FLOUR   1 TSP. GRATED ONION   PEPPER OR NUTMEG

SLASH THROUGH CORN KERNELS WITH A SMALL, SHARP KNIFE AND SCRAPE THE KERNELS FROM THE COB WITH THE BACK OF THE KNIFE. MELT BUTTER IN A SKILLET AND STIR IN ONION, CORN AND FLOUR. ADD SUGAR, SALT AND MILK. COVER AND COOK SLOWLY ABOUT TEN MINUTES. STIR IN CREAM JUST BEFORE SERVING. SPRINKLE WITH PEPPER OR NUTMEG.

(SERVES 6-8)   CORN PUDDING SCALLOP

2 C MILK   1/4 C MINCED ONION   2 CANS (16 OZ.)
1/4 C SUGAR   1 C CRACKER CRUMBS   CREAMED CORN
6 EGGS, WELL BEATEN   2 TBLSP. FLOUR   1/2 C BUTTER

MIX MILK, SUGAR, EGGS, ONION, CRUMBS AND FLOUR. BEAT WELL. STIR IN CORN. MELT 1/4 C BUTTER AND ADD. POUR INTO A BUTTERED SHALLOW BAKING DISH. DOT WITH 1/4 C BUTTER AND BAKE AT 350° 45 MINUTES. ALLOW TO SET A FEW MINUTES BEFORE SERVING. IF YOU LIKE, TOP WITH GRATED CHEESE AND/OR CHOPPED PARSLEY.

SPEEDY CORN RELISH   (1 1/2 C)

2 C DRAINED CORN KERNELS   1/2 TSP. SALT   DASH PEPPER
1/4 C CHOPPED GREEN PEPPER   1/2 TSP. DRY MUSTARD
1 SMALL ONION, CHOPPED   2 TBLSP. WINE VINEGAR
1/3 C SWEET PICKLE RELISH   2 TBLSP. CORN SYRUP
1/4 TSP. CELERY SEED   1 CANNED PIMIENTO, CHOPPED.

COMBINE ALL IN SAUCEPAN AND SIMMER 5 MINUTES.   REFRIGERATE.

141

CORN-TOMATO-PEPPER CASSEROLE (SERVES 8-10)

1 SMALL GREEN PEPPER	¼ TSP. PEPPER	2 C CHOPPED TOMATOES
½ C CHOPPED ONION	½ TSP. DRY MUSTARD	2 TSP. SUGAR
¼ C BUTTER	2 C MILK	1 C HERB STUFFING
¼ C FLOUR	2 CANS (1 LB.) WHOLE	CROUTONS
2 TSP. SALT	KERNEL CORN, DRAINED	2 EGGS, BEATEN

CHOP PEPPER AND SAUTÉ WITH ONION IN BUTTER UNTIL SOFT. ADD
FLOUR, SALT, PEPPER AND MUSTARD. COOK AND STIR UNTIL BLENDED.
GRADUALLY STIR IN MILK AND COOK UNTIL THICK AND SMOOTH. REMOVE
FROM HEAT AND STIR IN CORN, TOMATOES, SUGAR AND CROUTONS.
STIR IN EGGS. POUR INTO A GREASED 2 QT. CASSEROLE. BAKE AT
350° FOR 45-60 MINUTES. YOU MIGHT LIKE TO TOP THIS WITH
BUTTERED CRUMBS OR GRATED CHEESE.

YELLOW VEGETABLE CASSEROLE (SERVES 6)

1 C CORN (CUT FROM 2 EARS)	1 C CHEESE, GRATED
1 SMALL HEAD CAULIFLOWER, CUT UP	BROWN RICE (FOR 6)
½ HEAD CABBAGE, CUT UP	2 CLOVES GARLIC, MINCED
2 LARGE CARROTS, CUT UP	1 TSP. SALT 1 C MILK
1 SMALL ONION, CHOPPED	½ C WHEAT GERM
4 HARD BOILED EGGS, SLICED	ANYTHING ELSE YOU LIKE

PLACE VEGETABLES IN A CASSEROLE. SPRINKLE WITH SALT,
PEPPER AND WHEAT GERM. COVER WITH EGG SLICES AND GRATED
CHEESE. POUR MILK OVER. COVER AND BAKE AT 350° AN HOUR.
SERVE OVER COOKED RICE.

CORN OYSTERS (16 OYSTERS)

1 C SCRAPED CORN OR	2 TSP. GRATED ONION	¼ TSP. SALT
CANNED, CREAM-STYLE CORN	6 TBLSP. FLOUR	⅛ TSP. NUTMEG
2 EGGS, BEATEN	½ TSP. BAKING PWD.	3 TBLSP. BUTTER

MIX EGGS AND CORN. STIR IN DRY INGREDIENTS. MELT BUTTER IN
A SKILLET AND WHEN HOT, DROP IN TABLESPOONS OF BATTER. BROWN
ON BOTH SIDES. SERVE WITH MUSHROOM SAUCE OR MAPLE SYRUP.

DEEP FRIED EGGPLANT

BATTER — MIX WELL 1 1/3 C FLOUR, 1 TSP. SALT, 1/4 TSP PEPPER, 1 TBLSP. OIL AND 2 BEATEN EGG YOLKS. GRADUALLY ADD 3/4 C FLAT BEER. LET BATTER REST A COUPLE HOURS. BEFORE USING, ADD 2 STIFFLY BEATEN EGG WHITES. THIS WILL COAT 2 C OF 1/2" EGGPLANT STICKS. DIP EGGPLANT IN BATTER AND DEEP FRY (OIL AT 370°) UNTIL GOLDEN. DRAIN ON PAPER TOWELING AND SALT BEFORE SERVING.

MIDDLE EAST EGGPLANT (SERVES 6-8)

SAUTÉ IN OIL TEN MINUTES } 2 MEDIUM EGGPLANT, CHOPPED, 2 STALKS CELERY, CHOPPED AND 1 LARGE ONION, CHOPPED

ADD — 1 TBLSP. FLOUR AND 6 BEATEN EGGS.

ADD — 1/2 TSP. SAFFRON, 3 TSP. RAISINS, 1 TSP. SALT, DASH PEPPER AND 1/2 C NUTMEATS.

POUR — INTO A BUTTERED CASSEROLE. TOP WITH GRATED AMERICAN CHEESE AND BAKE AT 350° FOR 30 MINUTES.

SKILLET EGGPLANT PARMESAN (SERVES 6)

1 SMALL EGGPLANT, CUT IN 1/2" SLICES   1/2 TSP. BASIL
1 - 15 OZ. JAR MEATLESS SPAGHETTI SAUCE   6 OZ. SLICED MOZZARELLA
1/2 TSP. SALT   DASH PEPPER _ _ _ _ _ 4 TBLSP. PARMESAN _ _ _

MIX EGGPLANT, SAUCE, SALT, PEPPER AND BASIL IN A SKILLET. COVER AND SIMMER 20 MINUTES, UNTIL EGGPLANT IS TENDER, TURNING OCCASIONALLY. ARRANGE MOZZARELLA ON TOP AND SPRINKLE WITH PARMESAN. COVER AND HEAT UNTIL CHEESE MELTS.

EGGPLANT BOULANGE

SAUTÉ 3 CHOPPED ONIONS AND 1 EGGPLANT, CUBED IN 1/2" PIECES. ADD 1/2 C TOMATO JUICE, SALT AND PEPPER TO TASTE, 2 TBLSP. BROWN SUGAR AND CURRY PWD. TO TASTE. SIMMER UNTIL TENDER. ADD MORE JUICE IF NEEDED.

143

Sour Cream Noodles (SERVES 4-6)

8 OZ. (5½-6 C) EGG NOODLES

¼ C MELTED BUTTER	1 TBLSP. GRATED ORANGE RIND	1 C SOUR
½ C CHOPPED ALMONDS	1 TBLSP. GRATED LEMON RIND	CREAM
1 TBLSP. POPPY SEED	½ TSP. SALT	¼ TSP. PEPPER

COOK NOODLES AND DRAIN. IN A BOWL, MIX BUTTER, ALMONDS, POPPY SEED, RINDS, SALT AND PEPPER. TOSS WITH NOODLES. TURN OUT ON A HOT PLATTER AND TOP WITH DOLLOPS OF SOUR CREAM.

ONIONS ARE USED IN SO MANY DISHES AS A SEASONING, BUT WILL STAND ADMIRABLY ON THEIR OWN AS AN ACCOMPANIMENT TO MOST MEATS.

GLAZED PAPRIKA ONIONS (SERVES 8)

PEEL AND SLICE IN HALF CROSSWISE 4 LARGE MILD RED ONIONS (2 LB.) PLACE, CUT SIDE UP, IN A BAKING PAN. MIX ¼ TSP. SAGE, ½ TSP. EACH DRY MUSTARD AND SALT, ¾ TSP. PAPRIKA, 2 TBLSP. RED WINE VINEGAR AND 5 TBLSP. HONEY. POUR THIS OVER ONIONS. COVER PAN AND BAKE AT 350° ONE HOUR. BASTE A FEW TIMES WITH PAN SAUCE. UNCOVER AND DRIZZLE ¼ C MELTED BUTTER OVER. BAKE TEN MINUTES MORE — UNTIL GLAZED AND THE LIQUID IS EVAPORATED.

SCALLOPED ONIONS AND PEANUTS (SERVES 4)

3 C THIN SLICED ONIONS	½ C SOUR CREAM	¼ TSP. WORCESTERSHIRE
2 TBLSP. BUTTER	1-3 OZ. PKG. CREAM CHEESE	1 TSP. PAPRIKA
1½ TBLSP. FLOUR	½ TSP. SALT	½ C PEANUTS, CHOPPED
½ C MILK	2 HARD COOKED EGGS, MINCED	1 TBLSP. PARSLEY

PARBOIL ONIONS FIVE MINUTES. DRAIN. MELT BUTTER AND BLEND IN FLOUR. ADD MILK. BLEND SOUR CREAM AND CREAM CHEESE AND STIR IN, COOKING OVER LOW HEAT UNTIL THICK. ADD SEASONINGS AND EGGS. POUR IN A BUTTERED ONE QUART CASSEROLE. SPRINKLE WITH PEANUTS AND CHOPPED PARSLEY. BAKE AT 350° FOR 30 MINUTES.

Baked Stuffed Onions (SERVES 8)

8 MEDIUM RED ONIONS   1/4 c BUTTER   2 TBLSP. PARSLEY
1 C STUFFING MIX   1/4 TSP. THYME   HEAVY DUTY FOIL

PEEL ONIONS AND SCOOP OUT CENTERS WITH A SHARP KNIFE.
FINELY CHOP CENTERS AND MEASURE 1/4 C. TOSS STUFFING MIX
WITH 1/4 C ONION, BUTTER, THYME AND PARSLEY. FILL EACH
ONION WITH ABOUT 2 TBLSP. STUFFING. WRAP EACH ONION IN
FOIL AND BAKE AT 350° FOR 30-45 MINUTES.

ONION PIE

1 - 9" BAKED PIE CRUST   3 EGGS   1/8 TSP. PEPPER
8 SLICES BACON   1 C SOUR CREAM   1 1/2 TSP. CHIVES
2 C THINLY SLICED ONIONS   3/4 TSP. SALT   1/2 TSP. CARAWAY SEEDS

SAUTÉ BACON UNTIL CRISP; CRUMBLE. IN 3 TBLSP. BACON FAT,
SAUTÉ ONIONS UNTIL SOFT. BEAT EGGS SLIGHTLY AND STIR IN
SOUR CREAM, SALT, PEPPER, SNIPPED CHIVES, ONIONS AND BACON.
POUR INTO BAKED PIE SHELL; SPRINKLE WITH CARAWAY SEEDS.
BAKE AT 300° FOR 30 MINUTES. LET STAND A FEW MINUTES.

ONIONS AND PEAS ARE A FINE COMBINATION, AND MUSHROOMS AND/OR
SPROUTS. SERVE ONIONS WITH A CREAM OR CHEESE SAUCE, USING
EITHER AMERICAN OR SWISS CHEESE. TRY THE FOLLOWING WITH PORK:

Onion and Apple Casserole (SERVES 4)

6 MEDIUM ONIONS, PEELED   1/2 C SOFT BREAD CRUMBS
4 MEDIUM APPLES, PEEL AND CORE   3/4 C CONSOMME
8 SLICES BACON, SLICED   1/2 TSP. SALT

CUT ONIONS CROSSWISE INTO 1/8" SLICES. CUT APPLES THE SAME.
SAUTÉ BACON AND DRAIN ON PAPER TOWELING. IN 4 TBLSP. OF BACON
GREASE, TOSS BREAD CRUMBS. ARRANGE ALTERNATE LAYERS OF
ONIONS, APPLES AND BACON IN A GREASED BAKING DISH. COMBINE
CONSOMME AND SALT AND POUR OVER. TOP WITH BREAD
CRUMBS. BAKE AT 375° FOR 30 MINUTES, COVERED. UN-
COVER AND BAKE 15 MINUTES LONGER.

PEAS -

① COOK WITH A COUPLE OF <u>LETTUCE</u> LEAVES AND A TSP. SUGAR. WHEN BARELY TENDER, SEASON WITH SALT, PEPPER AND BUTTER.

② <u>MINTED</u> - FOR 1 PKG. FROZEN PEAS, COOK AS DIRECTED, ADDING 2 TSP. MINCED ONION, 1 TSP. DRIED MINT LEAVES. DRAIN AND TOSS WITH 2 TBLSP. BUTTER.

③ COOK PEAS IN CHICKEN BROTH AND STIR IN ½ LB. FRESH <u>MUSHROOMS</u> THAT HAVE BEEN SAUTÉED IN 3 TBLSP. BUTTER. YOU MAY ALSO ADD CHOPPED <u>RED PIMIENTO</u> AND/OR 2 TBLSP. <u>SHERRY</u>.

④ SAUTÉ ⅔ C CHOPPED <u>BACON</u> AND ¼ C MINCED <u>ONION</u>. ADD 2 PKG. FROZEN PEAS, 1 TSP. SALT, A DASH OF NUTMEG AND ½ C SLIVERED <u>ALMONDS</u>. COOK ABOUT 3 MINUTES — STIR IN ½ C HEAVY <u>CREAM</u>.

POTATOES —

ON "ADVENTURE" FOR <u>BAKING</u>, POTATOES ARE SCRUBBED AND PARBOILED UNTIL 3/4 DONE — THEN BAKED TO BROWN THEM UP FOR THE LAST ½ HOUR. SOMETIMES THEY'RE PEELED AND WHEN PUT IN THE OVEN, ROLLED IN BUTTER AND SPRINKLED WITH SEASONED SALT. AFTER ½ HOUR, POUR INTO PAN A CAN OF CHICKEN BROTH (FOR 8 POTATOES). BAKE AND BASTE FOR ½ HOUR MORE.

POTATO PANCAKES (6 CAKES)

2 SLICES BACON, DICE	1 EGG, BEATEN	1/8 TSP. PEPPER
2 C GRATED POTATOES	2 TBLSP. FLOUR	1/8 TSP. NUTMEG
1 SMALL ONION, GRATED	½ TSP. SALT	2 TSP. CHOPPED PARSLEY

IN LARGE SKILLET, FRY BACON UNTIL CRISP. REMOVE AND MIX WITH REMAINING INGREDIENTS. DROP BY SPOONFULLS INTO HOT BACON FAT AND COOK OVER MEDIUM HEAT UNTIL WELL BROWNED BOTH SIDES.

POTATO SOUFFLE (SERVES 4-6)

2 ½ C MASHED POTATOES	3 EGG YOLKS	1/4 TSP. PEPPER
1 TBLSP. GRATED ONION	3/4 C HEAVY CREAM	4 EGG WHITES
2 TBLSP. PARMESAN	1 TSP. SALT	

MIX ALL BUT EGG WHITES AND BEAT WELL. BEAT WHITES UNTIL STIFF AND FOLD IN. BAKE AT 350° IN A BUTTERED 1½ QT. DISH FOR 35 MINUTES OR UNTIL BROWNED AND SET.

MASHED POTATOES ARE SPECIAL WITH SOUR CREAM AND CHOPPED CHIVES
FOLDED IN. EXTRA SPECIAL— GARNISH WITH CHOPPED BACON.

SCALLOPED POTATOES

IN A BUTTERED CASSEROLE, LAYER THINLY SLICED POTATOES AND
ONION. SPRINKLE WITH SALT, PEPPER AND FLOUR. DOT WITH BUTTER.
REPEAT LAYERS UNTIL THE CASSEROLE IS FULL. POUR MILK IN TO
ALMOST COVER. (OR HALF MILK— HALF CHICKEN BROTH). BAKE AT 350°
FOR AN HOUR AND 15 MINUTES. TOP WITH GRATED CHEESE AND BAKE
15 MINUTES MORE.

SWEET POTATO PUFF   (SERVES 8)

6 YAMS OR SWEET POTATOES   1 C CREAM   ½ TSP. CINNAMON
4 EGGS, SEPARATE   3 TBLSP. SUGAR   ¼ TSP. NUTMEG
¼ C BUTTER, MELTED   1 TBLSP. GRATED ORANGE RIND

COOK POTATOES IN BOILING, SALTED WATER UNTIL TENDER. COOL AND MASH.
BEAT IN EGG YOLKS, BUTTER, CREAM, SUGAR, RIND AND SPICES. BEAT UNTIL
FLUFFY. BEAT EGG WHITES UNTIL STIFF AND FOLD IN. TURN INTO A GREASED
2 QT. BAKING DISH. BAKE AT 325° FOR ONE HOUR AND TEN MINUTES, OR
UNTIL PUFFED AND FIRM. GARNISH WITH ORANGE SLICES.

BRANDIED SWEET POTATOES

4 MEDIUM SWEET POTATOES   ¼ C RAISINS OR
2/3 C BROWN SUGAR   ½ C CHOPPED APPLE
¼ C WATER   ¼ C BRANDY OR
2 TBLSP. BUTTER   COGNAC

WASH POTATOES. DO NOT PEEL. BOIL IN WATER
TO COVER UNTIL BARELY SOFT. DRAIN, COOL AND
PEEL. SLICE INTO A GREASED CASSEROLE.
BOIL SUGAR, WATER, BUTTER AND RAISINS.
ADD BRANDY AND POUR OVER POTATOES.
BAKE AT 350°, UNCOVERED, 30 MINUTES.
BASTE NOW AND THEN.

147

SWEET POTATOES, ISLAND STYLE (SERVES 4)

6 MEDIUM SWEET POTATOES   MILK
1 TBLSP. BUTTER   2 TBLSP. BUTTER   2 TBLSP. BROWN SUGAR
½ TSP. SALT   ½ C GREEN PEPPER STRIPS   1 TBLSP. CORNSTARCH
⅛ TSP. PEPPER   1 DRAINED CAN (1 LB. 4 OZ.)   2 TBLSP. VINEGAR
PINCH NUTMEG   PINEAPPLE CHUNKS   ¾ C PINEAPPLE JCE.

COOK AND MASH POTATOES; ADD 1 TBLSP. BUTTER, SALT, PEPPER, NUTMEG
AND MILK ENOUGH TO WHIP POTATOES. IN SKILLET, SAUTE PEPPERS IN 2
TBLSP. BUTTER. ADD PINEAPPLE. COOK A COUPLE MINUTES. STIR IN
COMBINED BROWN SUGAR AND CORNSTARCH, THEN JUICE AND VINEGAR.
COOK, STIRRING, UNTIL CLEAR AND THICK. POUR MIXTURE INTO A 9" PIE PAN.
DROP SPOONFULS OF POTATO ON TOP. BAKE AT 400° UNTIL BUBBLING HOT.

RICE

STEAMED RICE IS SERVED WITH FISH — PERHAPS WITH LAMB.
WE LIKE TO STEAM IT IN A STOCK INSTEAD OF WATER.
VARIATIONS: HERB — MIX 3 TBLSP. CHOPPED PARSLEY, 2 TBLSP.
FINE CHOPPED CHIVES, ½ TSP. TARRAGON, ½ TSP. THYME AND
2 TBLSP. BUTTER WITH 3 C COOKED RICE.

     NUT — TOSS ½ C PINE NUTS OR TOASTED, SLICED
ALMONDS AND 3 TBLSP. BUTTER WITH 3 C COOKED RICE. YOU
CAN ADD A LITTLE GARLIC AND PARSLEY TOO.

     MUSHROOMS, BACON, GREEN PEPPER, ONION, RAISINS,
TOMATOES — THEY'RE ALL TASTY ADDITIONS TO A RICE DISH.
TRY SEASONING WITH CURRY OR SAFFRON FOR A CHANGE.

RICE AND PEAS

BUTTER 3 C HOT COOKED RICE AND TOSS WITH
3 C HOT COOKED GREEN PEAS. ADD 1 TSP. DRIED
TARRAGON AND 1 TBLSP. CHOPPED PARSLEY.
SPRINKLE WITH GRATED PARMESAN CHEESE.

Rice Pilaf

2 C RAW RICE	1 CAN MUSHROOMS	CAYENNE
1/4 LB. BUTTER	4 C BEEF BROTH	1/2 C CHOPPED
4 GREEN ONIONS	SALT AND PEPPER	PARSLEY

SAUTÉ RICE WELL IN BUTTER. ADD CHOPPED ONIONS AND COOK UNTIL ONION IS WILTED. ADD DRAINED MUSHROOMS. ADD BEEF BROTH (OR CONSOMME). STIR AND SEASON TO TASTE WITH SALT, PEPPER AND CAYENNE. POUR INTO A BAKING DISH. BAKE 30 MINUTES AT 400°. ADD PARSLEY, MIX AND BAKE TEN MORE MINUTES.

Curried Raisin Rice

2 1/2 C UNCLE BEN'S RICE	5 C CHICKEN BROTH
1 1/4 C CHOPPED ONION	1 TBLSP. SALT
3/4 C BUTTER	1 1/4 C RAISINS
1 TBLSP. CURRY PWD.	

BROWN RICE IN BUTTER WITH ONION. ADD BROTH WITH ALL SEASONINGS AND COVER. STEAM 25 MINUTES. STIR IN RAISINS.

Spanish Rice (SERVES 6)

6 SLICES BACON, CHOPPED	1 CLOVE GARLIC	1 1/2 TSP. SALT
1 C CHOPPED ONIONS	1 C RAW RICE	PEPPER
1 CHOPPED GREEN PEPPER	2 1/2 C TOMATOES	1 TBLSP. CHILI PWD.

SAUTÉ BACON AND DRAIN. IN DRIPPINGS, BROWN ONIONS, GARLIC AND GREEN PEPPER. ADD RICE AND COOK A FEW MINUTES. ADD BACON, TOMATOES AND SEASONINGS. COVER AND SIMER 20 MINUTES.

Apple Rice

SAUTÉ 2 CHOPPED ONIONS IN 2 TBLSP. BUTTER. ADD 2 C RAW RICE AND STIR FRY UNTIL GOLDEN. ADD 1 CAN CHOPPED WATER CHESTNUTS. POUR IN 4 C APPLE JUICE (HOT) AND 1 TSP. SALT. COVER AND STEAM 20 MINUTES. STIR IN 1 TBLSP. CHOPPED PARSLEY TO SERVE.

Rice Souffle   (SERVES 6)

1 C COOKED RICE	3/4 C MILK	1/2 TSP. SALT
2 TBLSP. BUTTER	1/2 LB. CHEDDAR CHEESE	CAYENNE
3 TBLSP. FLOUR	4 EGGS, SEPARATED	

MELT BUTTER AND STIR IN FLOUR. WHEN SMOOTH, STIR IN MILK
AND COOK UNTIL THICK. CHOP CHEESE INTO SAUCE AND COOK UNTIL
IT MELTS. BEAT YOLKS WITH SALT AND A DASH OF CAYENNE AND
ADD SLOWLY TO SAUCE, STIRRING. TAKE FROM HEAT. FOLD RICE
GENTLY IN. BEAT EGG WHITES UNTIL STIFF AND FOLD INTO SAUCE.
TURN INTO A GREASED 1 1/2 QT. CASSEROLE. BAKE AT 325° FOR
40 MINUTES. YOU MAY ADD 1 C CHOPPED, COOKED BROCCOLI OR GREEN
BEANS TO CHEESE-RICE MIXTURE BEFORE FOLDING IN WHITES.

SPINACH

IF YOUR SPINACH COOKS DOWN SO MUCH YOU'RE WORRIED ABOUT HAVING
ENOUGH, ADD ANY OR ALL OF THE FOLLOWING: MUSHROOMS, CHOPPED HARD
BOILED EGGS, CHOPPED WATER CHESTNUTS, CUT UP TOMATOES OR BACON BITS.

SPINACH MOLD   (SERVES 4)

3 TBLSP. BUTTER	1/8 TSP. PEPPER	3 EGGS, SEPARATED
3 TBLSP. FLOUR	1/8 TSP. NUTMEG	1 C COOKED, CHOPPED
1 TSP. SALT	1 C MILK	SPINACH, DRAINED

MELT BUTTER AND ADD FLOUR, SALT, PEPPER AND NUTMEG.
BLEND UNTIL SMOOTH. GRADUALLY STIR IN MILK
AND COOK UNTIL THICK. REMOVE FROM HEAT
AND ADD EGG YOLKS ONE AT A TIME, STIRRING
WELL AFTER EACH. STIR IN SPINACH.
BEAT EGG WHITES UNTIL STIFF AND FOLD IN.
POUR INTO AN UNGREASED 1 1/2 QT. BAKING
DISH. BAKE AT 375° FOR 40 MINUTES.
SERVE RIGHT AWAY.

Spinach Intrigue (SERVES 8)

2 PKG. FROZEN SPINACH   1/2 c MUSHROOMS
1/2 PINT SOUR CREAM   1/2 c BUTTER
2 SMALL CANS TOMATO PASTE   PAPRIKA
2 TBLSP. GRATED ONION _ _ _ _ _ _ _ _ _ _ _ _

COOK AND DRAIN SPINACH. SAUTÉ CHOPPED MUSHROOMS AND ONION
IN BUTTER. PLACE SPINACH IN CASSEROLE — ADD ONIONS AND MUSH-
ROOMS AND MIX LIGHTLY. SPREAD TOMATO PASTE ON TOP. COVER WITH
SOUR CREAM. SPRINKLE WITH PAPRIKA. BAKE AT 350°– 20 MINUTES.

Spinach Tart

LINE A 9" PIE PAN WITH PASTRY AND BAKE AT 425° FOR TEN MINUTES.
COOK 1 PKG. FROZEN SPINACH WITH 2 TBLSP. BUTTER, 1/2 TSP. SALT
AND A DASH OF PEPPER. DRAIN WELL AND MIX WITH 1/2 LB. COTTAGE
CHEESE, 3 EGGS (LIGHTLY BEATEN), 2 OZ. PARMESAN, 1/3 c HEAVY
CREAM AND 1/8 TSP. NUTMEG. SPREAD IN SHELL AND BAKE AT
375° FOR 30 MINUTES OR UNTIL SET. IT MAY BE MADE WITHOUT THE
PIE SHELL.

STUFFED SPINACH (SERVES 6)

2 PKG. FROZEN SPINACH   1 c PEPPERIDGE STUFFING MIX
1 PKG. LIPTON'S ONION SOUP MIX   3 TBLSP. MELTED BUTTER
1 PINT SOUR CREAM _ _ _ _ _ _ _ _ _ _ _ _

COOK AND DRAIN SPINACH. MIX TOGETHER ONION SOUP AND SOUR
CREAM. LET STAND 1/2 HOUR. MELT BUTTER AND MIX WITH STUFFING
MIX. COMBINE SPINACH AND SOUR CREAM MIXTURE. FOLD IN 3/4
STUFFING MIX. PLACE IN A BUTTERED CASSEROLE AND TOP WITH
REMAINING CRUMBS. BAKE AT 300° FOR 30 MINUTES.

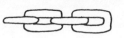

SQUASH

WINTER SQUASH (ACORN, BUTTERNUT, HUBBARD) MAY BE
BOILED, MASHED AND SEASONED WITH SALT, PEPPER AND
BUTTER. FOLD IN SOUR CREAM AND CHIVES FOR A TREAT.
   BAKED - PARBOIL ACORN SQUASH HALVES OR CHUNKS
OF HUBBARD UNTIL ALMOST DONE. SCORE FLESH AND
FILL CAVITIES WITH BUTTER, BROWN SUGAR (OR MAPLE
SYRUP) AND SPRINKLE WITH SALT. A NICE TOUCH ON
TOP IS TOASTED SLIVERED ALMONDS, CHOPPED PECANS
OR SALTED PEANUTS. BAKE AT 375° UNTIL GOOD AND HOT.
   SUMMER SQUASH (ZUCCHINI, CROOKED NECK, PATTYPAN) -
THIN SKINNED, AND IF YOUNG, THERE'S NO NEED TO PARE OR
DISCARD SEEDS. STRAIGHT OR CROOKED NECK AND ZUCCHINI ARE
GOOD RAW AND WHEN COOKED, THE FLAVOR IS BEST IF COOKED ONLY
UNTIL TENDER-CRISP.

GREEN AND GOLD CASSEROLE   (SERVES 6)

3 MEDIUM ZUCCHINI	3 EGGS, BEATEN	1/4 TSP. GARLIC PWD.
2 MEDIUM YELLOW SUMMER SQUASH	1 C MILK	1/4 TSP. OREGANO
1 MEDIUM ONION, CHOPPED	1 TSP. SALT	1/4 TSP. PAPRIKA
2 TBLSP. PARSLEY	1/4 TSP. PEPPER	2 TBLSP. BUTTER

CUT SQUASH IN 1/4" SLICES AND PLACE IN A 1 1/2 QT. CASSEROLE.
SCATTER ON ONION AND DOT WITH BUTTER. BAKE AT 400° FOR 15
MINUTES. COMBINE REMAINING INGREDIENTS EXCEPT PAPRIKA AND POUR
OVER SQUASH. SPRINKLE WITH PAPRIKA. BAKE AT 350° FOR 40
MINUTES OR UNTIL SET.

FRENCH FRIED ZUCCHINI (SERVES 4)

6 SMALL ZUCCHINI	1/2 C FLOUR
1/4 C EVAPORATED MILK	SALT

CUT ZUCCHINI IN LENGTHWISE STRIPS AS FOR FRENCH FRIED
POTATOES; DIP IN MILK, ROLL IN FLOUR. FRY IN DEEP FAT (375°)
ABOUT 5 MINUTES UNTIL GOLDEN. DRAIN AND SPRINKLE WITH SALT.

Zucchini Loaf (SERVES 6)

2 C GRATED ZUCCHINI   2 C MILK   CELERY SALT
1 SMALL GRATED ONION   1 C CRACKER CRUMBS   1/4 C BUTTER
2 EGGS, BEATEN   SALT AND PEPPER   PARMESAN CHEESE

MIX ALL TOGETHER EXCEPT PARMESAN, WHICH IS SPRINKLED ON
TOP. SEASONINGS ARE TO TASTE. PLACE IN A GREASED LOAF PAN
OR CASSEROLE AND BAKE AT 350° FOR AN HOUR. YELLOW
SQUASH OR CARROTS MAY BE USED IN PLACE OF THE ZUCCHINI (OR AS
PART OF THE MEASURE).

ZUCCHINI - TOMATO LAYERS

CUT UP IN A BUTTERED CASSEROLE: A LAYER OF SQUASH, A
LAYER OF ONION, A LAYER OF TOMATOES AND ONE OF CRACKER
CRUMBS. SEASON WITH SALT, PEPPER AND BASIL. DOT WITH BUTTER.
REPEAT LAYERS. BAKE AT 350° FOR 45 MINUTES.

SCALLOPED SQUASH

PLACE BARELY COOKED SUMMER SQUASH IN A GREASED BAKING
DISH. ADD A LAYER OF GRATED CHEESE AND 2 TBLSP. GRATED
ONION. POUR ON A MEDIUM WHITE SAUCE. TOP WITH BUTTERED
BREAD CRUMBS. BAKE AT 375° UNTIL BROWN - 25 MINUTES.

ZUCCHINI FRITATA (SERVES 4)

SAUTÉ A SMALL SLICED ONION AND A MINCED CLOVE GARLIC IN 2
TBLSP. OLIVE OIL UNTIL SOFT. ADD 2 C THINLY SLICED ZUCCHINI AND
SAUTÉ 3 MINUTES. IN A BOWL, BEAT 6 EGGS WITH 2 TBLSP. CHOPPED
PARSLEY AND SALT AND PEPPER TO TASTE. ADD TO ZUCCHINI AND
COOK OVER LOW HEAT UNTIL IT BEGINS TO SET. SPRINKLE 1/2 C
MUNSTER CHEESE ON AND DRIZZLE TOMATO SAUCE ON TOP. SLIDE
IN A HOT OVEN FOR A FEW MINUTES UNTIL CHEESE MELTS.

TOMATO SAUCE - 1 CAN STEWED TOMATOES (STRAINED). ADD: 1/2
CAN (6 OZ.) TOMATO PASTE, 1/2 TSP. SALT, 1/4 TSP. BASIL, 1 TBLSP.
ONION JUICE, 1/2 TSP. SUGAR. SIMMER FOR 15 MINUTES.

153

Tomatoes

ON THE SCHOONER, OUR SUPPLY OF FRESH TOMATOES IS USED FOR SALADS AND GARNISHING. CANNED PEELED TOMATOES AND STEWED TOMATOES ARE USED IN DIFFERENT WAYS — FOR SAUCES AND IN FLAVORFUL SIDE DISHES AT DINNERTIME TO ADD COLOR AND NUTRITION.

SCALLOPED TOMATOES (SERVES 4)

SAUTÉ 1 MEDIUM CHOPPED ONION IN 1/4 C BUTTER WITH 1 MINCED CLOVE GARLIC AND 1/4 C MINCED GREEN PEPPER. TOSS IN 2 C SOFT BREAD CRUMBS. ADD 1/2 TSP. SALT, 1/8 TSP. PEPPER, 2 TBLSP. CHOPPED PARSLEY, 1/2 TSP. DRY MUSTARD, 1 TSP. SUGAR AND 1/2 TSP. OREGANO. PLACE IN A BUTTERED CASSEROLE AND POUR OVER IT 1 # 2 CAN MASHED PEELED TOMATOES. SPRINKLE DRY BREAD CRUMBS ON TOP AND BAKE AT 350° FOR 30 MINUTES.

SIMPLE TOMATO STUFFING

USE ANY PACKAGE STUFFING MIX. PLACE IN A BUTTERED CASSEROLE AND POUR CANNED PEELED TOMATOES (CHOPPED) OVER THEM. MAKE THIS MIXTURE WETTER THAN THE PACKAGE DIRECTIONS FOR LIQUID. BAKE AS ABOVE.

TOMATO - CHEESE CUSTARD (SERVES 4)

1 CAN (1 LB.) TOMATOES   1 1/2 TSP. SALT   2 EGGS, BEATEN
1 TSP. MINCED ONION   1/4 TSP. PEPPER   1/2 C AMERICAN CHEESE
1 TBLSP. BUTTER   3 SLICES CRUMBLED BREAD

HEAT FIRST 6 INGREDIENTS. COOL, ADD EGGS AND MIX. POUR INTO BUTTERED 1 QT. CASSEROLE. TOP WITH GRATED CHEESE. BAKE AT 375° - 40 MINUTES.

154

TOMATO QUICHE (SERVES 6)

1 - 9" PIE SHELL   1/4 C MINCED GREEN ONIONS
4 EGGS, BEATEN   PEPPER   BASIL
1 C LIGHT CREAM   2 TBLSP. MINCED PARSLEY   SUGAR
1/2 TSP. SEASON-ALL   3 MEDIUM TOMATOES   SALT

BAKE PIE SHELL AT 425° FIVE MINUTES. MIX EGGS,
SEASON-ALL, ONIONS, PEPPER AND PARSLEY. POUR INTO
SHELL. ARRANGE TOMATO HALVES IN A CIRCLE AROUND EDGE
OF PIE. SPRINKLE CUT SURFACES OF TOMATOES WITH BASIL,
SUGAR, SALT AND PEPPER. BAKE AT 350° FOR 50 MINUTES
OR UNTIL SET. THIS MAY BE MADE WITHOUT THE CRUST.

TOMATO OYSTERS   (SERVES 4)

1 CAN (1 LB.) TOMATOES   1 EGG   1/2 TSP. WORCESTERSHIRE
1 SMALL ONION, MINCED   3/4 TSP. SALT   DASH TABASCO
3/4 C SOFT BREAD CRUMBS   1/4 TSP. PEPPER   DASH CAYENNE

DRAIN ALL LIQUID FROM TOMATOES AND CHOP PULP. ADD
REMAINING INGREDIENTS AND MIX WELL. DROP BY TBLSP. INTO
HOT BUTTER IN A SKILLET AND BROWN SLOWLY ON BOTH SIDES.

MOM'S TOMATO PUDDING (SERVES 4)

1 1/4 C TOMATO PURÉE   1/3 C BROWN SUGAR   1/4 C BUTTER,
1/4 C WATER   1/2 TSP. BASIL   MELTED
1/4 TSP. SALT   1 C SOFT BREAD CRUMBS

HEAT TOMATOES AND WATER TO A BOIL AND ADD SALT,
SUGAR AND BASIL. PLACE BREAD CRUMBS IN A BAKING
DISH AND POUR MELTED BUTTER OVER THEM. ADD THE
TOMATOES, COVER AND BAKE AT 375° FOR ABOUT 30
MINUTES.

Vegetable Notes